Amelia Watchman

All I want for Christmas ISN'T you

Tamarillas Press

To my darling husband for all your support, our two girls for all the inspiration, nothing goes unused. Also to my mum, sister and auntie for all your help and encouragement, I couldn't have done it without you all.

Other books by Amelia Watchman

Romantic Comedy:
Love, Hate and Indifference

Children's Book:
There's a Dragon in my Garden

Chapter 1

Would he even notice if I got up right now and left? Would he even care? What about if I threw something at him? Probably just dodge and continue what he's doing. He'd deserve it if it hit him though.

I appraise him while he stares straight ahead at the television screen, engrossed in a cheesy Christmas movie. They're at the bit where they have their happily ever after. Beautiful Christmas trees surrounding them, it's snowing, they've realised they love each other and everything is perfect. Where's my happy ever after?

It's the same every night. I look down at his body, lean and strong and with a spattering of stubble over his face. The stubble is longer than normal, no effort made there. I grit my teeth, swallowing down the anger and the urge to shout. What's the point? I try to push the feeling down and take a deep breath.

He suddenly turns his head; he must have sensed me scrutinising him. I look away and stare down at my own body. Poking at the extra pounds that sit softly around my middle, I sigh loudly. I wasn't always like this. I used to be a bit of a gym bunny or maybe more of a gym mouse, if that's a thing. I'd scurry into the gym trying to remain undetected and avoid conversations, go about my business. Warm up on the running machines, some weights, maybe a bit on the elliptical machine and bikes, all dependant on what was free. Then scurry out. I was in good shape then. Not so much now.

'You okay? What are you doing?' he asks, searching my face, his eyes suddenly showing concern. But it's too little, too late.

I turn my attention to Spence as he pads into the room and jumps up onto the sofa next to me. I stroke him, trying to calm my nerves. Such a good dog, his fur so soft, always here to comfort me.

Jake doesn't even know what he's done.

I feel the anger start to bubble up again and I try to swallow it down. I'm not going to tell him. Stroke, stroke, stroke. He should know. Stroke, stroke, stroke. It's not like it's a difficult date to remember. I look down at Spence who gazes up at me with his big brown eyes, at least someone loves me. Even if it is a silly, old collie.

He came as part of the package deal when Jake and I married. Jake's mum had him from a pup but he took so much to Jake that when he moved out the dog came too. His mum has one of those Bichon Frise dogs now, so cute but yappy, always at your ankles.

'Fine,' I answer flatly. Which clearly means I'm *not* fine. Everyone knows that. I wait for him to say something else but instead he turns his attention back to the telly, apparently satisfied with my answer. He lifts his legs and places them on the coffee table. My *new* coffee table, to add insult to injury. I splutter and cough at the audacity of it and he slowly places his feet back on the floor, pointedly staring straight ahead. I don't know how many times I've asked him not to do that. He knows it drives me crazy. Everything goes quiet and there's just the noise of the TV. I sit and wait for something, anything to happen.

'I've got a few quotes I need to go out for tomorrow morning,' he suddenly quips. In his line of work, he's often out quoting.

'Okay, I'm over Marnie's anyway.' I shrug, not really caring what he's doing with his day. Glad to not be spending it together.

'Who's going to walk the dog then?' he snaps accusingly.

'Well you could do it when you get back from the quotes,' I snap. 'How many have you got?' My tone is ready for a fight. I could explode at any minute; why's he testing me right now?

'Oh okay, that's fine. Just a few. I'll walk him.' He huffs. 'Will you be there all day?'

'Maybe,' I say noncommittally.

'Well it would be nice if you could let me know.'

'Why? Have we got any plans?' I search his face for clues. Has he planned a surprise for tomorrow? I dare to feel excited.

'No, I just thought perhaps we'd pop in and see Mum for a bit.'

Jake's mum is hard work, the polar opposite of my mum, she's very stern and can be quite a difficult woman. Not very friendly and inviting, the last thing I really want to do is go and see her.

'Well you don't need me. You go.' I force a smile.

'Is this that rubbish, about her not liking you again?' he whines. 'I've told you a million times, that's just her personality, it's what she's like. Don't take it personally.'

I sigh, tired with it all. How can I not take it personally? She always makes sly digs at the state of the house, she's never worked a day in her life and it's beyond her why my home is sometimes a bit messy. He opens his mouth but then closes it again, perhaps thinking better of continuing down this path. He can't even be bothered to have a real fight.

'I'm going to bed.' I get up, disturbing Spence who scurries over to Jake; traitor.

Jake looks over briefly and nods. Perhaps he doesn't want to anger the beast anymore or perhaps and more likely, he doesn't care.

∞ ∞ ∞

I lie in bed seething, waiting for him to come up. Going over all the things I should say to him. But I won't. I'm too cross. I can't believe he's forgotten our anniversary. We've been married seven years. December 21st, a beautiful winter wedding. So close to Christmas, I never thought he would forget. It was one of the long-standing jokes at the wedding. It's not that long ago, we're well past the honeymoon period but surely, we shouldn't be at old married couple status yet? We've not even hit ten years.

I glance at the wedding photo on our bedside table. It was captured during the speeches, candid, that's what they call it, a beautiful candid shot. Jake is standing, gesturing to me while I laugh and raise my glass, the soft curls framing my face perfectly. He looks proud and happy. What happened to that man?

And look at me, I was so full of joy, so in love and so sure of myself but not now. I hardly recognise myself. I look at Jake in his soft grey suit, the smile on his face isn't something I have seen a lot recently, I realise sadly. Nowadays we're like ghosts of our former selves, moving slowly through this world but not so much together anymore. Snapping occasionally at each other.

Our wedding was so personal to us, small and intimate, only our closest friends and family. Just twenty people. A quick wedding in the registry office and a roast in our friend's barn which we'd painstakingly decorated for days before. I'd picked up my dress at a local charity shop, it was a stroke of luck. It fitted so perfectly it could have been made for me. I finished it off with a soft, white, fluffy winter bolero. I felt divine. There was a light snow that Christmas, it couldn't have been a more gorgeous winter wedding.

Every detail of that day is etched onto my mind, including the choice I made. I thought it was the right decision but sometimes I wonder. How different would my life have been if I'd chosen another path?

I think back to our last anniversary before everything happened. Flowers in the morning, a candlelit dinner, romance. It was wonderful. I always used to get so excited for our anniversary and then Christmas but my Christmassy mood has gone this year. Evaporated. We went through the motions of putting the Christmas tree up but it doesn't look right, it doesn't feel right. Not with everything that's happened.

I sigh and roll over. Thinking about the card and gift hidden in my chest of drawers. Well he's not having it if he can't even say happy anniversary. Arsehole. I toss and turn, struggling to drift into sleep.

Finally, I give up and head to the kitchen for a glass of water. Stomping through the living room on my way, brushing past the Christmas tree and sending needles all over the floor. I'm desperate to get his attention, but Jake doesn't even flicker, his attention seemingly turned to something else on the TV. His feet back up on my coffee table. I could spit with anger. Spence is sitting at his feet whilst he softly strokes him.

I clatter and bang in the kitchen, loading the dishwasher and tidying up the kitchen as I go, my anger fuelling me. No point in trying to be quiet for him.

As I walk back through the living room, I notice Jake's gone to bed, just a few crumpled crisp packets in his place. Slob. When I get into the bedroom, I can hear Spence's soft snore and Jake's laboured breathing. I can't quite believe Jake's already asleep. It only fuels my anger further.

I groan deeply, I'm so tired now but I doubt that sleep will come so easily to me. I walk around to my side of the bed and go to climb in but Jake has cocooned himself in the covers. They're firmly wrapped around him and clamped in between his legs. To add insult to injury he's in the middle of the bed, his knees on my side. Leaving nothing for me.

I'm infuriated. He's opened the window as wide as possible and I can feel a strong, cool breeze wafting in. If you're hot, why wrap yourself up in the duvet? It's winter, we don't even need the window open. It makes no sense to me and has been a bone of contention with us for years. I consider shaking him awake or dropping his gift on him, but I don't. I close the window and approach Jake's resting body. I start to pull. Gently at first, but those legs are strong and he has the covers in a vice-like grip, there's no budging. Well I'm not sleeping without any covers. If anyone deserves to be cold, it's him.

I start to simultaneously pull the covers and push his knees back with my foot. I'm perplexed that he hasn't woken up, I don't see how anyone can sleep through this. After a lot of shoving he finally starts to shift and I give him a final big push. This push finally awakens the beast and he goes to turn over, all the pushing has clearly moved him a lot further over in the bed than anticipated and he tumbles onto the floor. He makes quite a sound as he goes down. Thump.

'What the...? What happened?' he says, confused, looking around the room.

I muffle a laugh, climb in and pull the duvet over me, tucking it tight underneath me. I don't say a word but I can hear he's awake now, panting from the shock. I keep my back to him, making my point yet again. I try to keep my breathing even so he thinks I'm asleep and at some point, I hear his soft, slow breathing. I'm still awake, staring at the ceiling but eventually I fall into a dreamless slumber.

Chapter 2

I sleep in late and I'm pleased Jake has already left when I wake. Now I don't have to have an uncomfortable breakfast with him. I pad downstairs with Spence on my heels desperate to go for his walk but I've only got half an hour before I need to be at Marnie's. I search under the tree for the carefully wrapped presents for Penny and Dana, smiling to myself at the thought of them ripping these apart the second I get there.

∞ ∞ ∞

I knock softly on the door afraid of waking any sleeping babies and wait. It takes a while for Marnie to answer the door and when she does, she looks a mess, her clothes are all skewwhiff and her hair is in a messy mum bun. Dana's sitting snugly on her hip and Penny's shuffling behind her, dressed only in a pair of pyjama bottoms.

'I don't want to wear a dress! Dresses are stupid,' Penny wails, as I enter the house. I kiss Dana on the cheek and go forward towards Penny as she backs away and runs to the living room.

'Don't say stupid.' Marnie sighs. 'Go through into

the living room.' She gestures to me, rolling her eyes at the situation. 'Look Lena's here now. Why don't you come over and give her a cuddle and a kiss? Say hello,' Marnie instructs but Penny's having none of it. She folds her tiny arms over her chest.

'No,' Penny whines.

'Sorry,' Marnie mouths to me but it doesn't faze me. Afterall I have a secret weapon.

'Oh, that's such a shame you don't have any cuddles and kisses for me, because I have this lovely present here for you but if you can't even say hello. Well...' I say calmly, shrugging at the supposed shame of it all.

Penny inches closer, the strop seemingly forgotten. 'Is it in there?' she asks, pointing at the bag. 'It's a big bag.' She grins.

I nod, smiling. She comes over and wraps her little arms around me.

'I'm happy to see you, Auntie Lena.' I'm technically not her auntie but Marnie and I are so close she has always referred to me as her aunt.

I take her little hand and we walk further into the room and sit down on the soft rug. Clearly this isn't the first present Penny has opened. I look around and am greeted with an explosion of toys and wrapping paper all over the floor. The Christmas tree is looking a bit worse for wear, half of the tree looks to be undecorated.

Marnie sees me looking at it. 'I know.' She rolls her eyes again. 'We've had to put all the tree decorations up high; Dana just keeps on pulling them down and trying to eat them. She almost pulled the tree over on herself yesterday. And Penny, well, she's opened some of the presents that were under the tree this morning. Didn't you? Santa isn't going to be very happy with you, is he?'

Marnie turns her attention back to me. 'I'm going to have to rewrap them all.'

Penny looks up sheepishly and I can't help but laugh. She's such a little cherub. Penny's always had a mischievous streak and I love her for it.

'If Santa didn't want me to open the presents, why did he put them under the tree?' she quips, not missing a beat.

'Those were presents *I* had wrapped for other people, not for you and Santa's doesn't come 'til Christmas Eve. Anyway, there will be no presents under the tree until then, now.'

Penny starts to show me some of her new toys, bored of the conversation with her mum and the big bag of presents forgotten for now. Even though it's not Christmas yet she's received a few gifts from friends and family who won't see her on the "big day" itself.

'Where's Mitch today?' I ask but I already know where he is.

'He's in the office. He's very stressed at the moment. You'd have thought he was about to take a whole year off the way he's been going on. It's only two weeks for goodness sake.' Marnie half smiles but I can see this has all been a strain on her.

'For goodness sake,' Penny echoes, Marnie glares at her daughter who turns her attention back to her presents.

Poor Marnie, I can see everything has really taken its toll on her. I resolve to help her out more, I know how challenging Penny can be at times, the little sassy madam. Added to that, Dana wasn't planned and since she's been born Mitch has tried to take more and more on in the office. He's keen to make sure that Marnie doesn't have to go back to work and they can stay in their beautiful (albeit expensive) home. It's in one of the richer parts of town, all massive newbuilds. I've always really coveted it but Jake and I could never afford somewhere like this. Marnie confided in me she'd rather move somewhere smaller and have him around more but he won't hear of it, so she feels a bit stuck.

'How's everything with Jake?' Marnie asks, but before I can answer there's another knock on the door.

'I'll get it,' I say, half pleased for the opportunity not to speak about him.

∞ ∞ ∞

Jeanie's standing at the door looking very bohemian in a beautiful flowing dress and long patterned coat. Her hair is long and wavy in a half up, half down do that looks like it took her no time at all to do, and probably didn't. It would take me hours to get that kind of look. I find my hand going to my hair and smoothing it down.

'You look lovely,' I say, taking her all in.

'You too.' She smiles, starring pointedly at my jogging bottoms. I do not look lovely but hey I don't care, who am I trying to impress anyway?

We walk through into the living room, where Penny jumps up ready for more gifts.

'Hi Auntie Jeanie, do you have some presents for me too?' She grins, like butter wouldn't melt.

'Yes, but you're clearly not ready for them. You're not even dressed.' Jeanie gasps, putting her hands on her hips. Penny pouts, sticking her bottom lip out.

'Shall I take you to go and get dressed?' I ask Penny, at least Marnie might get five minutes to speak to Jeanie in peace.

She nods, smiling. 'But I'm not wearing a stupid dress,' she says pointedly, looking at Marnie who rolls her eyes again.

'Fine, wear what you want,' Marnie sighs. 'But you're wearing one on Christmas day or I'll tell Santa to come collect your presents.'

∞ ∞ ∞

Penny's bedroom is a little girl's dream come true, all pink flowers and princesses. Marnie decorated it before Penny was born imagining a little girly girl. Instead she got Penny who's wild, funny and most definitely a tomboy. Her favourite colour is blue and she loves dinosaurs, dragons and dirt.

'Right, what do you want to wear?' I ask. She's chosen what she wears since she was two years old and so it comes as no surprise to me when she starts pulling out her clothes and selecting what she will wear. A green top and blue leggings, it's low down on the excitement-o-meter for clothes but it's very Penny. She's true to her own style, I'll give her that.

'I'm going to be four soon,' Penny informs me, as if I don't already know. She's actually going to be four in three months but I can't see the point in correcting her.

'Hmmm, but it's Christmas first.'

'I know. I love Christmas.' She hops around the room trying to pull her trousers up. 'Do you love Christmas?' she asks me and instead of answering her straight away I give the answer some thought. I used to, but not so much now.

'Yes.' I nod along.

'Does Uncle Jake love Christmas too?' she asks.

12

'Yes, I suppose,' I answer, but I've not given much thought to how he feels about it this year. Although he clearly doesn't give much thought to me either.

'Shall we go downstairs?' I ask Penny as I watch her start to pull out her toys, five minutes up here and the room will look as bad as the living room.

'Yes, soon. I have a surprise for you.' Penny giggles to herself.

'Oh yes, what's that?' I'm really hoping it's not as good as her last surprise for me which was some snot on one of my favourite jumpers.

Penny opens the ottoman that sits at the end of her bed and starts to throw all the teddies out, evidently looking for whatever my surprise is.

'Penny, I think we shouldn't get all the toys out,' I say helplessly, thinking of poor Marnie having to re-tidy it all.

'Okay,' she agrees, but still continues in her pursuit. Suddenly she stands up with something crumpled in her hands, she puts her finger to her lips. 'Shhhh, don't tell Mummy.'

I'm intrigued now, it's probably one of Penny's drawings; she loves to colour and draw and hide the pictures all over the house. 'What is that?'

'Shhhh, it's magic.' Penny comes over and presents it to me.

Inside her hands is a half-sized cracker, it looks like it's already been pulled. 'Is that a cracker?'

Penny nods and proceeds to hold it out to me. 'Pull it with me, this one's a magic one.'

I tentatively put my hand out and grab hold of one end, it looks like it could just fall apart as it is but I can see that Penny has taped it back together. I wonder if Marnie knows that she has this.

'I fixed it from my arts and crafts box,' Penny admits, clearly so proud of herself.

I laugh to myself; Penny is such a bright spark. She could speak so well so young, and with her being so petite, people would often marvel at her. She's a real chatterbox and Marnie always jokes about how she's a good talker because she has a lot of practice.

'Okay,' I say, wondering what's inside. 'Shall we pull on three.'

Penny nods.

'One, two, three.' It doesn't take much pulling for the cracker to come apart and that's when all the sequins that Penny has obviously stuffed inside come spilling out all over her floor. I gasp.

'What's all this?' I ask, thinking how annoyed Marnie's going to be.

'It's the magic.' Penny grins. 'Don't worry it knows what you want. You don't have to tell me.'

I laugh. 'We'd better tidy up or Mummy's going to be mad.' I help Penny stuff her teddies back in the ottoman.

'You go on downstairs now and I'll hoover up,' I say to Penny.

As I drag the hoover across the floor one piece catches my eye, it's not a sequin like the rest but a little green Christmas tree. I pick it up and put it in my jogging bottoms ready to give to Penny later, she could use it on one of her Christmas cards.

∞ ∞ ∞

Back downstairs and the present unwrapping is in full force. There's wrapping paper everywhere and Dana is happily munching on a piece. Penny and Dana have

14

already unwrapped Jeanie's and I can see they're chomping at the bit to have mine now.

'There you go girls,' I say giving them my gifts and settling down on the sofa with Jeanie and Marnie. A doll for Dana and a giant dinosaur for Penny.

'So, how's everything with Jake?' Jeanie asks.

'Same old,' I reply sadly.

'You know you guys are just in a rut, why don't you try going out or doing something special together. More time together would surely help?' Marnie suggests.

I know she's trying to be helpful but I don't want to hear it.

'He forgot our anniversary,' I say, deadpan. 'I don't want to spend more time with him right now. And we've still got Christmas to get through.'

Jeanie gives me a little pat on the arm. 'It won't always be like this or feel like this,' she says, giving me a kind smile but she doesn't really understand what I'm going through.

'How about you?' I ask Jeanie, trying to deflect the conversation from my sad life. 'Are you still seeing that guy?' I can't remember his name, there have been quite a few guys over the last few years but none of them have stuck so I've found it hard to remember their names.

Jeanie raises her hand dismissively. 'I dumped him. He was getting very serious and everything he did annoyed me. I suddenly realised I was dreading spending Christmas with him and that wasn't right so, I ended it.'

'Oh, I'm sorry,' Marnie says, placing her hand on Jeanie's arm. Jeanie shrugs her off.

'It's okay, it's better it's over now and then I can meet someone that's more suited to me.' Jeanie smiles.

'How's work?' Jeanie asks turning to me, changing the subject. I suppose it's kind they've not mentioned the elephant in the room but it doesn't mean it's far from my mind. It's always there waiting and sometimes it would be nice if they asked. They're good friends and I know I could bring it up but it's not always easy to know where to start or what to say.

'Same old,' I say dismissively. Everything in the office is fine but I'm unchallenged, unable to take the next step and I suppose stuck in a rut there too. So many ruts.

'You should find a new career,' Marnie suggests.

'She's right, best thing I ever did leaving there,' Jeanie agrees.

'I know, Jeanie, but you were meant for bigger and better things. What else could I do? I'm in my thirties, now isn't the time to be looking for a new career. I should be settled in, climbing the ladder.' The idea of starting over is depressing.

'It doesn't have to be like that.' Jeanie rolls her eyes at me. But how hard would it be to start again. Not everyone can decide to up and travel all over the world to find themselves.

'I never really imagined you working in an office like that, surely insurance isn't your calling?' Marnie smiles kindly.

'Well no, but how many people get to do what they really want to do? And besides I have no idea what that is.'

I have no idea about a lot of things. Apparently.

Chapter 3

I wake early in the morning but can't get back to sleep. My head is full. Full of worries I can't seem to push away and I lay there succumbing to them, letting the fears engulf me. Thinking over everything that Jeanie and Marnie said. Should I change career? What's wrong with Jake and I?

I look over at Jake, his body rhythmically rising up and down. I'm consumed with jealously, why is it so much easier for him? Spence is at the end of our bed snoring away, having sneaked up from his bed. My heart fills, he's such a sweet boy. Look at that, I prefer my dog to my husband.

Finally, the alarm goes off at six and I'm shattered. Now I feel like I could sleep all day, typical. Spence's head lifts to see what all the movement is about but the lazy dog drops his head back down to sleep, nestling further into the bed.

I heave myself out of bed and into the shower before Jake can surface, keen to avoid him as much as possible. I hear him crashing around in the kitchen making cups of tea as I shower. I wrap myself in a huge towel and patter along the hallway into the bedroom to get dressed. He has left his side of the room in a huge mess; yesterday's pants and clothes are all over the floor and the bed remains unmade. I shuffle around collecting his clothes and make the bed, sighing at the laziness of it all.

Finally, I look around the room my eyes stopping on the ceiling which has cracks running all over it. I sigh, one of many jobs we're going to "get around to", but never do. I always thought the house was quite shabby chic, but now I see the shabby, but not quite the chic. I pick up Jake's towel from last night and pelt it into the wash basket, it's only a mere foot away but why should his majesty have to do it when he has muggins here?

I glance in the mirror; my eyes have huge bags under them. Perfect. As I have time, having leaped out of bed instead of snoozing the alarm, I apply a full face of make-up. I take my time and quite enjoy it; I wonder if Jake will notice. I look pretty good. I don't normally wear much make-up in the office so I feel a bit special. It feels nice to make a bit more effort, I put red lipstick on and style my hair down and straight. I team it up with my best work clothes. A white blouse and black knee length, fitted skirt. The skirt's a bit snug around the waist but I think I can just about get away with it. It digs in when I sit down but I sit behind a desk, so no one will notice. I finish it off with my imitation Jimmy Choos, I love these shoes, if only they were real. Sigh. I'd have to win the lottery.

I clip, clop downstairs. Jake is sitting at the kitchen table loudly crunching his cornflakes. Spence is wrestling his food bowl over in the corner, I keep my eyes off the mess. If I don't see it, I won't have to tidy it up. When I enter, he momentarily looks up but then turns his attention straight back to his food.

'Morning,' Jake says brightly. Evidently, he's fine

with me now or is trying to put a brave face on it. He's not one for arguments. Well I'm still annoyed. He hasn't said anything about our anniversary over the whole weekend. I wonder if he'll forget Christmas too. Now wouldn't *that* be convenient.

'Morning,' I say, waiting for him to notice my outfit and the obvious effort I've made. Normally I scrape my hair back and throw on some black trousers so this is certainly stepping it up, but I get nothing. He doesn't even look at me.

'What time are you going in?' he asks. Well at least he's noticed I'm up earlier than normal, I think grimly.

'I'll have some breakfast and leave shortly after,' I say. 'Could you take Spence out?' I ask, knowing full well he's not leaving for work until 9am today, he's meeting the others on site. Jake is a tree surgeon, it's the reason he still looks so great, while I get fatter and fatter by the day. It was one of the things that really endeared me to him, a man of nature, an outdoors man. Whenever I told any of my girlfriends what he did they were suitably impressed. The great thing about his work was that he started early, but generally finished early too. Which means he's around a lot. It was nice in the beginning, not so nice now, he's always under my feet and making a mess.

I go over to the kitchen counter and begin to pour myself a bowl of cornflakes and join Jake at the table.

He groans and wipes his face. 'Suppose, I'll have to.' I can sense his irritation. I normally always take Spence for a walk in the morning then he hops on Jake's truck and spends the rest of the day out and about with him. Being an old dog he's no hassle and he's so well trained we know he'll do as he's told.

Occasionally, depending on the job, Jake will leave

him at home but taking him is one of the perks of working outside. He doesn't really need much walking, so I don't know why Jake's getting annoyed about it.

'I was going to fix one of my chainsaws,' he whines, taking another huge mouthful and crunching down loudly. I wince at the sound, anger bubbling away, has he always been such a loud eater?

'Well, I need to be in early for an important meeting,' I snap. I don't but I'm pissed off now. It's not asking a lot for him to walk his own dog.

'I wondered why you were dressed like *that*,' he says, gesturing at me rudely.

What's that supposed to mean? I leave the rest of my cereal and get up quickly, screeching my chair over the hardwood floor.

'I've got to go,' I say heading towards the door, I'm furious. He can't even bring himself to say I look nice. At the door I turn on my heels. 'Happy anniversary for Saturday, by the way,' I almost shout, slamming the door behind me. Jake's mouth bobbing open behind me. What a great way to start the day.

∞ ∞ ∞

My office is a thirty-minute drive away and I arrive at 7.30am, usually I'd be in just before 9am. Maybe I'll be able to get away early I think, knowing full well that I won't. The office is large and open plan, there are a few private offices but they are reserved for the 'big bosses' as we all call them. Although, they're windowed so we can all still see what's going on in there. They have blinds to close for privacy but they rarely ever do. If they do, we all know that means something bad, last year they let a few people go and the blinds were closed the whole week, the atmosphere in the office bordered on hysteria.

As I walk past the private offices, I can see Fran working away. I bet she's been in since 7am, she's the head of strategic account management here at Morgans. She's a big deal and can be quite intimidating if she wants to be. Fran's dressed in one of her most prominent power suits, a navy-blue number with a hot pink shirt, it would look ridiculous on most people but she pulls it off. I wonder who's she's taking down today. Her hair is in a tight bun pulling her face up, giving her the look of a face lift, not that she needs it. She's only 29. She's gesturing wildly whilst on the phone and does not look happy. I keep my head down and walk quickly past. I'm working on a project with her at the moment and I pray it's nothing to do with that.

I hurry over to my desk desperate to sit down, the walk from the car to the office has already started to make my toes throb. I'm reminded why I don't wear heels often now. I sit down and take my shoes off under the desk. That's better.

'Well, well, well. You look like a right dog's dinner. Who are you trying to impress?' Eli sneers, blatantly looking me up and down. Eli, my colleague and a friend of sorts.

'Shut up, no one,' I say, staring daggers at him. Eli has no filter, so whatever thought pops into his mind comes straight out of his mouth. He can be a real laugh but also a real bitch.

'Well, you do look nice,' he soothes, sensing he may have missed the mark with his first comment. 'You should wear make-up more often; you don't look so pale or tired.'

'Great, thanks,' I murmur. 'Do you know what's going on with Fran? Who's she talking to?' I ask changing the subject from my appearance. I don't need any more backhanded compliments.

'Oh, HR, I think. You remember the new guy was supposed to start ages ago? Fran's furious he's not here yet, she wants him in now. He must be *amazing*.' Eli speaks in hushed tones but his theatricality means it's hard for the entire office not to watch him. He's talking about our new manager, the role has been vacant for months, Eli and I both went for it, but neither of us got it. We're waiting to see the *wonderful* person who did. Need to work on my confidence and practice my interview questions was my feedback. Well I thought I was perfect for the job and I spent ages practising, so I don't know what more I can do. I think back to my conversation with Jeanie and Marnie, if I can't climb the ladder here, where I've worked for years, what hope do I have anywhere else?

'I don't understand why they don't let him wait until after Christmas now? It's a funny time to start.' I shrug my shoulders wondering what he's really going to do now?

Eli shrugs. 'I think he should have been in around a month ago but there were some issues with his security checks. They might even already be paying him. Fran would hate that. He'll have to work twice as hard now to make him worth his money,' he sneers.

∞ ∞ ∞

Two hours later and Fran is doing the rounds around our department with an unfamiliar man, he's tall compared to Fran, who's five-feet nothing, but he's probably just average height. He has a friendly face, dark hair and glasses that don't frame his face well. I'm already giving him a makeover in my mind.

Eli catches me staring. 'That's him you know. Our new boss.' He nods his head towards him. 'Don't look too hard, he's clearly gay.'

I shake my head. 'You think that about everyone. I was just wondering who he was. Thanks for clearing it up,' I say to Eli, deadpan. I'm not much in the mood for office politics today. I can't help but be impressed by Fran, that call to HR obviously did the trick, I bet the person on the receiving end was shitting bricks.

Fran finishes introducing the new manager to the more senior members of the team and it's our turn next. She marches over quickly with him striding behind her to keep up.

'This is Kian, he's the new accounts manager and your new line manager. Kian these are your team members Eli and Lena. They'll be able to catch you up on everything that's been going on.' And with that Fran turns quickly and heads straight back to her office. Duty complete, no need for idle chitchat. I bet she's lost a lot of time having to march him around the office and can't wait to get back to her own work now. She's such a workaholic.

'Nice to meet you,' Kian says, with a soft Irish accent. It's lovely and gives him a boyish charm. He's dressed in a smart grey suit and blue tie.

'Yeah, you too,' Eli replies flatly. Poor Kian doesn't even know what he's got himself into. 'Have you just moved to the area?' Eli brightens, he may be pissed off that he didn't get the job but it won't reel in his inherent nosiness.

'No, I've lived here for a while, my partner is from

Twinton.'

Eli eyes me at the word partner, maybe he was right this time.

'Oh, is *he*, what's *his* name. Maybe I know him?' Eli practically sings while smiling at me.

'*She* is called Steph and I doubt it,' Kian says. I stifle a snigger, Eli has turned bright pink, he readjusts his glasses clearly trying to think what to say next. It's not very often he is left speechless; I can't take my eyes off Eli, his mouth bobbing whilst he tries to recover.

'Well, shall I show you the project we've been working on?' I ask, changing the subject to rescue Eli.

'That would be perfect,' Kian agrees.

Kian sits down at my desk and we start to go through the work we've been doing over the past few weeks.

∞ ∞ ∞

A few hours later and Fran is in a meeting with Kian when Dom walks in, he's the Director above Fran and actually helped get me this role in the first place. We've been friends for a long time, he's incredibly handsome and once upon a time maybe we could have been something. I've found myself day-dreaming more and more about that *once upon a time* recently.

'Oh, here he is.' Eli purses his lips. He barely sees him but has taken quite a dislike to Dom. We don't have much to do with him in our role so he really doesn't know him. 'International playboy.' He's just jealous. Dom seems to have a different girlfriend every month but why not when he's a bachelor, he's just dating. He hasn't found the right woman. I'm sure it would be different if he did.

Dom comes over to my desk which is very unlike him. 'Hello, Lena, you're looking lovely today,' he says.

I offer Dom a small smile. I suddenly feel shy but I'm pleased finally someone notices and compliments me and not in a backhanded sort of way either. Eli snorts into his drink and I have to use all my energy not to roll my eyes. I know exactly what he's thinking and it won't be complimentary, but he's wrong about Dom. I know him. Eli thinks he's a closet homosexual and that's why he can't settle down, but he thinks that about everyone. Wishful thinking.

'Could you meet me in my office in ten minutes?' Dom asks, checking his watch and offering a warm smile. He waits for my answer even though it wasn't really a question and I nod my head, suddenly worried about what this could be about.

We watch as Dom walks away, his well-fitted suit is clearly expensive and his hair is styled perfectly; in a different life he could have been a model. He enters his huge office and draws the blinds.

Shit.

Chapter 4

'What do you think all that's about?' Eli asks, nodding his head towards Dom's office. I don't know but now I'm anxious. It's rare we get called into Dom's office and the closing of the blinds is not a good sign. I hope I'm not getting sacked. That's all I need, more time at home with Jake.

Seems off that Dom would do it rather than Fran but maybe he thinks it would be better coming from him and it wouldn't be fair for Kian to do it, imagine that on your first day. Unless I've made a huge mistake. I start to try to calm myself, thinking myself into my happy place but it's no use. I'm glad it's not long before I need to go into the office,   so I don't have time for my imagination to spiral.

'Well you never know, maybe the international playboy is looking for something a bit closer to home.' Eli smirks, raising his eyebrows and laughing at his own joke.

This time I allow my eyes to roll.

∞ ∞ ∞

I cautiously knock on Dom's office, I'm very aware that

everyone is watching me right now. Eager to see the outcome. It's like watching a car crash, you can't help but look even though you really shouldn't.

'Come in, come in,' Dom booms brightly. I enter the room quietly closing the door so as not to draw any further attention. His personal office is the biggest in the building, he even has a small leather sofa in it which he is currently sitting on. I hesitate, looking over at his desk and the chairs either side and then to Dom. It seems odd to sit over there if he's going to fire me, I'd rather he did it at the desk. Although thinking about it, wouldn't HR be in here? I look around the room hunting for Hugh from HR, as though he might be hiding under the desk.

'Come, sit,' Dom says, sensing my hesitation and patting the seat next to him. We've been friends for years; I don't know why I'm feeling so awkward. Probably because he's about to fire you, says a little voice in my head. I shake my head to try and push those thoughts away. Dom gives me a puzzled look and waits for me to sit down.

'Is everything okay? Have I done something wrong?' I ask, worried I've let him down. Dom was so helpful getting me this job a few years ago, he even helped with some interview questions and is always there to talk to. When he's in the office that is. I suppose that's normal if you head up a medium-sized company like this, always here, there and everywhere. His life must be so much more exciting than my dreary life.

'No, don't be silly. It just occurred to me we've not seen each other much recently, with me away in the London office, and I wanted to see how my friend is getting on.' Oh, well, that was unexpected. It feels nice to have someone care and ask how I am. I think back

to the past few months and I can't think of a single
time that Jake has asked that simple question. In such
close proximity I can smell Dom's aftershave, he smells
divine and I fight the urge to lean in closer and breathe
him in. Keeping the scent with me all day. God, he
looks sexy, was he always this sexy?

'Well, you know.' I shrug, trying to push my
thoughts away. 'Things are okay, I guess.' It's hard to
pretend to him, he can tell when I'm lying and I don't
really want to lie to him.

'Everything going well with work?' Dom asks,
brushing his hand through his sand-coloured hair.

'Oh yes, why has somebody said something?' I begin
to worry that this meeting is a precursor to something.
Perhaps Fran has said something about my work on the
project. I've checked it so many times, I know it's spot
on, unless I missed something. I begin to rack my
brains. Did I miss something?

Dom begins to chuckle. 'Always thinking, you.' He
smiles. Dom knows all too well I can be a bit of a
worrier. 'No one has said anything. As far as I'm aware
you're getting on well. You really should have got that
manager role. I routed for you but, I'm afraid, it was
two to one.' Dom was on the interviewing panel for the
job and he gave me the feedback, which was kind. I
really thought I had it this time. I came out excited that
I'd answered everything, their nodding heads made me
feel like I'd done really well, but I was so wrong. Kian
obviously did better.

'How's your mum?' Dom asks, changing the subject.
It's sweet of him to ask. I bet he already knows the
answer, our mums are round each other's houses
several times a week, well they do live next door to each
other. I think they always secretly hoped we'd end up

together, they were almost right.

'Yeah, not bad, you know Mum, extravagant as ever. Still misses Dad but she's getting on well. She retired this year,' I say, feeling guilty I haven't been over there in a while. I just can't face her at the minute. Not with everything that's happened.

'Yes, terribly sad your Dad's gone. How long's it been now?'

'About two years,' I say, feeling the sadness that he's not here anymore wash over me. It comes in waves, or so they say.

Dom nods. 'He was a great man,' Dom kindly changes tack. 'Jake, treating you well?' Dom and Jake have never been the best of friends but they tolerate each other, probably for my sake. They're just very different. I could never imagine Jake working in an office, he can just about open a spreadsheet, never mind use formulas, or doing presentations. He'd never know where to start. They're like chalk and cheese, Jake and Dom, so very different.

'Yes, everything's fine on the Jake front,' I say, not wishing to lose face.

He gives me a long look before speaking. 'He's a lucky man, Jake. Are you okay? You look great but a little…' He pauses and looks to me for reassurance, unsure how to finish the sentence but I know what he's saying. I look sad. Because I am. Trust Dom to notice.

His kindness at noticing has left me speechless and I find myself beginning to cry. I don't know if it's Jake or Dad or just everything. Dom looks at me and wipes the tear from my eye with his thumb. It sends tingles down my spine. We're in such close proximity that the gesture feels really intimate and only makes me cry harder. I can't remember the last time I was intimate with Jake. It's probably been months. Dom places his big arms around me and I sob into his shoulder for a while, a dark pool forming on his expensive navy suit.

'I… I…I'm… j… just… b…being… silly,' I mumble, feeling ridiculous. He'd only called me in to see how I was, I bet he wasn't banking on me sobbing all over his leather sofa and lovely suit.

'He takes you for granted, you know,' Dom almost whispers, looking deep into my eyes. 'He doesn't even know how lucky he is.' He bites down on his lip as if he has something else to say and I can feel the butterflies start to swim in my stomach. I don't want him to stop. I want to hear what he has to say.

I look up to him waiting for it. 'What is it? You can say it.'

He looks into my eyes but doesn't say anything. He searches my face and I sit still, letting him. Then he leans forward, placing his lips softly onto mine. I can feel his trepidation but it's so good to feel wanted, to feel seen, that I don't pull away. Even though I should.

I move in closer, testing the waters, waiting to see what happens. Hungry for his kiss. Longing for him. I breathe in his smell. He notices my response and his kiss changes, becoming more rapid and urgent. His hand drops onto my skirt, feeling at my leg and I feel myself leaning in to him.

As his hand sneaks higher, I suddenly come to my senses. What am I doing? I pull away. I'm married. To Jake. I made my bed and now I must lie in it. This is no way to behave.

I wipe the kiss away with the back of my hand, my lips feel bruised from the intensity and I can see a smear of red lipstick on Dom's face. 'I should go. I don't know what I'm doing,' I say, trying to shake some sense into myself.

'I'm sorry, I couldn't help myself.' Dom looks earnestly into my eyes. 'You're just so amazing,' he starts, but I lift my hand to silence him. I don't want to hear anymore. I participated in the kiss just as much as he did, I wanted the kiss and now I have to live with that. Live with the guilt. Do I tell Jake? Would he even care?

A hundred things are running through my mind. What does this mean? I try to calm my face down, ready for the show on the other side of the door. I've been crying so everyone will think something has happened. It probably would have been better if I had been sacked. If I wasn't already married this could be so different. I'm so confused.

∞ ∞ ∞

I walk out of Dom's office. I try to hold my head high but I know my eyes will be puffy from crying. I clip clop as quickly as possible to the ladies. There's an eerie silence you don't often get in open plan offices. I can feel everyone starring as I dodge around the many plastic Christmas trees that sit around the office.

I can see people are dying to know what's happened. The office rumour mill will be on overdrive after this. Well, you'll never guess. If I can just get through the next few days then we'll all be off for Christmas and hopefully it'll be forgotten about by then. Someone's surely going to get drunk at the Christmas party and do something inappropriate or embarrassing. I have my fingers crossed. Then I'll be yesterday's news.

I can still feel the remnants of the kiss from Dom on my lips, I bet I have no lipstick left on them now. I can't believe it; Dom and I have been friends for so long but I never saw that coming. He's always been so lovely to me but I didn't think he saw me that way.

I thank my lucky stars no one is in the ladies and shut myself away in the cubicle, praying no one will come in under the guise of checking up on me. We'll both know they're really trying to find out the gossip.

My temple starts to throb with all the worries buzzing around in my head. What have I done? Does this mean it's over with Jake? Over one little mistake? Do I want it to be over with Jake? I know I'm not happy. Is that why I did it? Do I want to be with Dom? Would he even want to be with me? Maybe I am just another notch on his bedpost, but it didn't feel like that.

I can feel myself start to sob again. At this rate I'm going to have to stay in here until everyone goes home. It's only 11am, that's not going to work. How will I cope with the rest of the day in the office? Maybe I can pretend I'm feeling unwell and leave. I feel the panic begin to rise in my chest, I need to do something or they'll find me gasping on the bathroom floor. I don't need that. A hospital trip would definitely trump a Christmas party drunken embarrassment.

I start to tap my feet, rhythmically counting the tap, tap, taps. One, two, three. Desperate to calm myself. The cubicle is small and feels stifling but thankfully well-maintained and clean. I think about my breathing, I wish I had a bag right now, I close my eyes and think of my happy place. Back seven years to my favourite garden, a simpler time, before decisions were made.

Wrong decisions?

Chapter 5

I open my eyes, finally feeling calmed. I think I can go out and face everyone now. My breathing has evened out and if I splash a bit of cool water on my face it may alleviate some of the puffiness around my eyes. Better to get back out there now and put a stop to the spinning rumour wheel. The longer I'm here, the more it turns. Who knows what they've concocted in all this time? I'll probably have a team of people around my desk as soon as I get out there.

I walk cautiously out of my stall, hoping I can have a few minutes at the sinks before I have to speak to anyone. Thankfully it's empty. I clip clop to the sinks and turn the cold tap on, dabbing the water near my eyes, careful not to ruin my make-up.

I peer at my face. I'm a little red but really not too bad at all. I don't know how but my hair seems to look better than this morning. It even has a slight curl to it that, if I didn't know better, I would say had been done on purpose. Surprisingly, despite most of it appearing to be on Dom's face when I left the office, my lipstick is still intact. My skin is looking almost sun-kissed, it must be the lights or perhaps I'm still flushed from earlier. Eli might be right, I think reluctantly, I should wear make-up more often if it makes this much difference.

No wonder Dom kissed me, I reason, then chastise myself for thinking such thoughts. What's Jake going to think? It's not a laughing matter.

I hesitate as I head over to the door, readying myself for the onslaught of questions. As I take a step, I feel something under my heel, that would be just my luck to leave the toilet with a big wad of tissue paper under my shoe. I look down but nothing's there, I lift my shoe up to see the faux red patent soles and there, stuck to the bottom of my shoe is Penny's green tree sequin sparkling. How odd, it must've fallen out of my pocket. I pick it up, ready to stuff it into my handbag.

I try to think of my happy place again and breathe slowly. My head begins to throb like I've run into a door at full pelt. I can do this. They don't know what happened with Dom. I will not cry, especially if someone asks me the dreaded question… are you okay? I walk out of the toilets with purpose, my head focused towards my desk. If I can just get there, I can busy myself with work before anyone has the chance to pounce. Only a few more days left in the office, then the Christmas party to go and then I'll be off until the new year. I could get out of the Christmas party, perhaps I'll catch the flu. It's so common over the winter. I could sow the seed now, a few strategic coughs and splutters.

I hurry over and am so glad to see Eli must be on one of his many juice breaks. Even though he's as thin as a piece of paper he's always on some health kick or another. The flavour of the month at the moment is juicing. Last month it was weights at the gym, but I've not heard much about that recently. It just seems a convenient way for him to skive off for half an hour while he makes his juice from the "finest ingredients" of course, or else why bother. Or so he tells me.

I open my palm ready to pop the tree sequin away but it's gone. I look back towards the toilets but decide against going to look for it, me on my hands and knees by the loos is hardly a way to draw attention away from myself.

I get comfortable and for the first time allow myself to glance around the office. Everyone is getting on with their work, there's the usual murmur of activity. Everything seems normal. Maybe this afternoon won't be so bad. Maybe I can quietly get on with my work and then go home. I can feel a few people glancing in my direction but there's no questions, not the usual inquisition.

Ctrl, alt, delete and I tap my password into the screen. The spinning wheel whirls round and round and then a message pops up saying my password is wrong. I must've typed it incorrectly. I try again but the same message appears. What is going on? I'm starting to panic again. I can't keep my head down and avoid everyone if I can't do my work. I'll have to call IT and then I'll be sitting here for hours while they "get round to it at some point, probably today". Normally this wouldn't be so bad. It just means hanging around and gossiping at other people's desks, but when you're the source of the gossip, surely not so fun.

I try one more time, tapping slowly and steadily. SPENCE200. I know that's my password and it doesn't need changing yet. I can see Eli starting to head back, a giant, fresh juice in hand. Great.

I start to open my drawers for a good rummage to make myself look busy. It's funny but the top drawer looks a lot tidier than I remember. I tentatively open the bottom draw and to my surprise there are lots of chocolate bars, all different sorts and a few discarded wrappers. Did someone put these in my desk for me? Kind of sweet, but I could do without the rubbish. Even if they ate one, I wouldn't know if they'd taken the wrapper with them. I smile to myself and begin to look around, I wonder who did it? That's quite nice. I'm not particularly close to my work colleagues, I prefer to keep it professional at work. I don't socialise that much outside of work either but it's kind that someone is trying, someone's noticed.

Eli approaches my desk, looking hesitant. Here we go.

'Everything alright, Lena? Did you need something?' he asks, looking puzzled and gesturing at the drawers.

'Yes, fine thank you,' I say, closing them quickly. I doubt it was him who put the chocolates in, he wouldn't really think of that. Especially with all his healthy eating and living. I don't want a lecture when I didn't even put them there.

'Okay, well could I have my desk back?' he asks softly, popping his juice down on the corner of the desk. His desk? This is my desk? Oh my God, have I been sacked and Eli has already moved into my desk. Wow, talk about jumping in someone's grave. I'm suddenly furious with it all. With Dom.

'Your desk? This is my desk. Yours is over th…' I stop mid-sentence, as I go to point, I notice that the desks aren't quite where they normally are. The office looks quite different in fact, I don't know why I didn't notice before. Gone are the cheap Christmas trees dotted around and bought by the different teams in the office, in their place is a single tree, tastefully decorated in the centre of the office. It looks nice. Classy. Gone is the tinsel on the computers. Fran is sitting in what would normally be Eli's desk and it's filled with her paraphernalia.

I look on my desk, my pictures of Jake, Spence, Penny and Dana are gone, there's nothing on my desk. Where are they? Okay, what's going on? Is this some kind of practical joke?

Eli is looking at me like I'm a mad woman. I'm trying desperately not to freak out and cause a scene. My head is spinning, I'm not sure what to do. In my haste to get up so Eli can have what is seemingly *his* desk back, I knock his precariously placed juice over. A full glass of purpley-red, lumpy liquid goes all down my legs and all over my shoes and onto Eli's snakeskin boots. Everyone in the office gasps. Great. Just what I need. More attention.

Eli covers his mouth, seemingly horrified and I wait for him to rip it out of me. I'll probably be paying for those shoes, ugly as they are. I've probably done him a favour really. I wait for the onslaught of bitchy comments but they don't come.

'Oh my God, your shoes, Lena. I'm so sorry. Are you okay?' What's he sorry for it was my own fault for being so clumsy. 'I should have placed it somewhere else.'

'No, no I'm sorry, Eli.' He looks at me with surprise. 'It was my fault,' I say, he should be able to put his juice on what is clearly his desk, after all.

'No, it was mine,' reassures Eli. 'I shouldn't have put that drink there.'

I scratch my head, now I really am confused. I think I've heard Eli apologise once, and if there's ever a doubt about whether it's his fault, he would never take the blame, unless it was one of the big bosses. This is so weird. All the commotion has garnered the attention of the rest of the office and Fran has come rushing over. She's dressed really peculiarly today, looking decidedly frumpy for her and very drab. Normally she's business suits and colour, so today is very out of character. Her mousey hair is normally tied up in a smart bun or styled to within an inch of its life, but today it's all down, looking lank and lifeless. I've never seen her looking so dull, she's aged about ten years.

'Let's go in your office and get you cleaned up,' Fran says, gesturing for me to come with her. 'Maybe you have other shoes in there?'

My office?

I let Fran lead me, keeping my mouth closed but looking around in wonder. Did I hit my head? Am I dreaming? My shoes are swimming with Eli's juice and I can feel them squelch with every step.

I get into Fran's office still feeling fuzzy headed and confused by the events of the last ten minutes. What is happening with everyone? I sit down on the chair opposite the desk. Maybe I've fallen asleep in the toilets. Well Dorothy, we're not in Kansas anymore.

'I'll go get you some wet wipes, I think I have some in my desk. Give me your shoes and I'll see what I can do,' she instructs. On her way out through the door she pauses. 'Such a shame, these Jimmy Choos are so lovely.'

Jimmy Choos? Fran helping clean them?

Alone, I look around the office. There's not much in here to tell me whose office it is, but Fran seems to think it's mine. I go around to the other side of the desk looking at the computer screen and seeing my username. This is so weird what is going on? I tentatively type in my password. The wheel whirls but the error message comes up again. Sigh, so I still need to speak to IT.

I start to look around the room. On the desk is a great big bunch of flowers. I look at the card, I'd never dream of doing that in Fran's office, but surely that's okay if it's *my* desk? My head throbs.

L, Happy anniversary! Your loving husband. I'll see you tonight to celebrate. Xxx

Is L me? Jake doesn't normally call me L. These flowers are beautiful though. In whatever weird world I've fallen into he has done very well. What is happening to me? Have I gone crazy? Me, the big boss? Whatever this dream is, I kind of like it. I run my hand along the big, expensive desk. I marvel at my huge office; it's very stylishly decorated. Not dissimilar from how Fran's was, but somehow more expensive, more high end. The desk is central to the room with a huge brown leather chair which looks more comfortable to sit on then my sofas at home. I smile to myself. On the other side sit two huge cream chairs, which also look rather plush, they remind me of the chairs in old 1920s mansions but they're clearly a lot newer than that. To the side of them sits a beautiful Christmas tree.

I start to pace around a bit more confidently, there are no pictures on the walls though, no real clues for me to soak in. Who is *this* Lena? She seems wonderful. I must be making a lot of money here in this dream world to have my office kitted out like this. It all seems pretty wonderful right now and I make a resolution right here to enjoy it. While it lasts. It's only a dream. I already know I'll be disappointed when I wake up.

There's been so little joy in my life why not see how the other half live? I'm sure I could do this job, if I really put my mind to it. Sure, it's quite a few pay grades above where I currently am, but how hard could it really be?

Fran re-enters the room with a packet of wet wipes. 'You never know when these will come in handy,' she says, offering them to me.

I look at Fran, she's practically a shell of her former self. I don't imagine the normal Fran keeping wet wipes to hand just in case they're needed. I start to mop at my legs and my head spins, I think I'm going to be sick.

'Are you okay? You've gone very pale.' Fran looks at me with concern. I don't know who this kind-hearted Fran is but she's not the usual hard-ass I know. Whatever's happened, I rather like it.

Chapter 6

'I'm not feeling that great,' I say by way of an explanation. I feel as though I've entered another dimension. How crazy will I look if I start insisting Eli is sitting at my desk? I laugh to myself at all the chocolates hidden in his drawers. Well that explains his fad dieting. He's a secret eater and I never knew.

I think back to all the times he shamed me when I had a piece of cake on someone's birthday or a chocolate bar of my own. Making comments about how I'd put on weight and I should try whatever he was into. All this time he had all of that squirreled away. The cheek of him. When does he eat them though? I've rarely ever seen him eat anything apart from salads or whatever else he's into at the time.

Fran interrupts my thoughts, 'Well, we have a meeting in about five minutes, do you think you're well enough for that? It's not a long one. You don't need to do much,' Fran says dismissively, waving her hand.

'But my shoes.' I gesture at them sitting sadly over the other side of the office, stuffed with tissue.

'I have some spare shoes in my drawer,' Fran offers, scurrying out of the room to retrieve them. I guess I'm staying for this meeting then.

I slip Fran's trainers on, the ones she occasionally uses to walk to work. They've definitely seen better days and they're ruining the look of my lovely outfit.

'Remind me who we're meeting?' I say to Fran, as we walk to the meeting room and I pray I don't look completely useless.

'Pearson and Sons. You've just got to do the beginning presentation and then it's all discussion. I don't think it'll be more than half an hour.' She smiles but I can already feel the dread creeping over me. A presentation? I suddenly feel sick again.

Presentations have never been my forte, at university during the first presentation I ever gave, I froze completely. I stood there for five solid minutes, which felt like an eternity. It was excruciating. I opened and closed my mouth so many times until my professor finally put me out of my misery and told me I could try again next week. I came back to it and read from a piece of paper; it wasn't the most thrilling presentation but I managed it. But here I have no notes, I don't know what I'm supposed to be presenting on. I want to sit down and put my head between my legs. I try to calm my mind by inhaling deeply.

Once in the meeting room I fuss around trying to set the slides up, thank God they're already on Fran's computer.

'Is it the one labelled Pearson and Sons?' I ask.

'That's it.' Fran smiles before checking the teas and coffees and that the room is set up how she likes. I'm relieved to see it's a presentation that I have actually seen, even if I've never given it before. I've been with the company long enough; surely I can muddle through? I click through trying to refresh my mind. Yes, I think I can do it. Just don't freeze. Think, think. I try to reassure myself but I can feel the sweat building. I open the window, I'm boiling. Fran stops what's she's doing and runs over.

'It's freezing in here. We can't have the windows open,' she says and closes them. I start to try and visualise my happy place, to get my breathing under control. I'm feeling so hot I wish I could run outside. Before I have a chance, Pearson and Sons enter.

'Hello, Lena.' They smile, coming over to take my hand, their gaze lingering slightly on my untidy trainers.

'Hello err Mr Pearson.' I realise I don't know their names and smile tightly whilst Fran greets them by name, 'Mark, Gavin, John,' she enthuses. They're obviously very familiar and she even makes them laugh. Great.

I bring up the presentation and take my place at the front. Hello and good morning, hello and good … I run the start of the presentation through my head over and over trying to let it sink in so I don't sound completely stupid.

Hello and good morning, Hello and good morning. 'Horning.' I trill loudly once everyone is seated. Fuck. Did I just say horning? I stifle a giggle at myself and realise, as I look at the faces around me, they did not find it the least bit funny. This has not broken the ice. The no-sense-of-humour-parade is here. My armpits feel sticky and I can feel my top lip starting to sweat. I try to dab at in inconspicuously with my sleeve.

'I'm going to talk to you about our wonderful company, Morgans and why you should choose us,' I say with a bit more decorum. I'm pleased with myself. Perhaps it won't be so bad.

Before I can go any further Fran butts in. 'They've already chosen us, remember, Lena.' She smiles tightly, nodding. 'That's the wrong presentation, it's the other one. I'm so sorry it's completely my fault and my bad labelling.' Fran rescues me and everyone gives a little laugh. She shrugs. 'I always know what everything is, but it can be difficult if you're not in my mind.' She clicks open a folder and finds another presentation labelled Pearson and Sons. I can't help but feel irritated. Did she let me load up the wrong one deliberately?

I watch as Fran loads up the presentation, quickly flicking through it to check it's right this time and I know I've not seen this one before. I feel the sweat beginning to drip down my back. I busy myself taking a sip of water and try to compose myself whilst Fran gets everything ready and then I retake my seat at the front.

I don't know what to say. I'm completely at a loss. My mouth bobs up and down and I wipe my brow as Mark, Gavin, John and Fran stare intently. I look at the slides but it's no use, there's hardly any text. After what feels like forever but is probably five minutes, I admit defeat, I can't present this.

'I'm so sorry,' I say. 'I'm really not feeling too well today.' It's not a complete lie.

'Shall I do this one for you?' Fran asks kindly, to my rescue yet again. 'Lena you're definitely not yourself, are you okay to stay?' she asks appraising me. I can't imagine the Fran of my world ever asking if I'm okay and I look at her in wonder. Who is this kind Fran? In this dream world she's so much nicer and caring. She'd never have helped me but would have humiliated me and then probably sent me out. I'm grateful to her, she's rescued the situation and the clients are now nodding along happily.

'Yes please, if you don't mind Fran giving the presentation, that would be wonderful,' I say in my most professional voice, which sounds a little bit like the Queen. 'I'll be here though, in case there are any questions. I'm so sorry.' I nod to Pearson and Sons, as if I could answer anything. I sit through the next hour-and-a-half presentation. Half an hour, my arse. Fran simultaneously takes all of the questions and the clients seem happy with everything when they leave, albeit a bit awkward.

∞ ∞ ∞

After the clients have left, I go over to Fran.

'I'm feeling really poorly now. Sorry about the presentation, you did it really well,' I say hanging my head low. 'Do you think you could drive me home?' I ask cautiously. 'I'm not feeling well enough to drive,' I explain.

Fran gives me a bit of a puzzled look but nods in agreement. I'm not entirely lying because I do feel really exhausted and peculiar, but when your whole world changes completely and without explanation, who wouldn't? And in this dream world I don't know what I drive, or even if I have driven here so I don't want to search the car park for hours. It's hard enough finding my real car sometimes and I know what it looks like.

∞ ∞ ∞

I fold myself into Fran's tiny Kia Picante and I'm astonished that everything has changed so much for Fran as well as for me. Perhaps not in such a good way for Fran, but she seems like a much nicer person. So perhaps it is in a good way. All the power has obviously gone to her head in real life and so she's incapable of

45

being nice. It was so great she took over in front of the clients, she must think I'm crazy. The Fran I know wouldn't have even registered my juice incident, never mind got me something to clean it up, much less cleaned my shoes. I think back to the time I fell over at work, Fran couldn't get out the way quick enough. Leaving everyone else to deal with me, even though she was the most senior person there.

'Got any plans this weekend?' I ask her, trying to make small talk on the way home, but really trying to pry more into her life. I'm fascinated.

She smiles tightly, and fidgets in her seat. 'Well it is Christmas, but just a quiet one for me.'

'Of course.' Christmas, how could I forget. 'Are you not with your family for Christmas? No boyfriend?' I pry, I know I shouldn't but I realise I don't really know much about Fran. We've only ever really talked about work so it's kind of interesting to see another side to her.

'Not really,' she answers noncommittally, looking away. 'My family live up north.'

'Really? I never knew that. You don't have an accent. Just someone special then?' I grin at the thought of her with someone, she never really seems interested in anyone. Except herself of course.

'We moved down here when I was young, but my parents recently moved back,' she explains, avoiding the other question. I decide not to pursue the point any further, she clearly doesn't want to tell me her life story and I put myself in her shoes. Well I was in her shoes mere hours ago and I realise I wouldn't want to tell my boss too much either. Perhaps she's just split up with someone and I've put my foot in it. I hope I've not offended her. As we drive on my eyes start to feel really heavy and I close them involuntarily, I feel as though I could sleep for days.

∞ ∞ ∞

'We're here,' Fran trills, waking me from my slumber. We're where? I look around, not recognising anywhere. I'm outside a large house sitting on a massive driveway. Do I live here? The house is set back from the road and has large conifer trees lining the driveway, keeping it lovely and private. The trees are adorned with Christmas lights, it must look amazing at night. I'm astonished I've woken back up still in the dream. Is that even possible?

I wipe the drool from the corner of my mouth.

'Thank you, Fran, I'm so sorry I fell asleep. I don't know what's got in to me,' I say, slipping my still slightly slimy shoes back on. At the door I search through my handbag and find a set of keys. I fumble around whilst Fran waits on the driveway. I wish she would just leave but she's clearly checking I get in okay. I drop the keys several times pushing the wrong key into the door lock. I try to focus on the task at hand. Why are there so many keys? What are they all for? Finally, I hit the right key and I'm in. Hurrah.

I walk into a beautifully decorated hallway. It's a soft shade of green that would have been hard to find. I know this after decorating our spare room green, it took me ages to find the right shade and then when it was all that colour it matched Kermit the Frog. Jake took the piss out of it for weeks, but refused to let me redecorate it. We have to live with it now, he said not to waste any more money on it when we hardly use it. He took the opportunity to say I told you so though of course, he'd wanted to keep it neutral but I insisted on colour.

I wave off Fran, desperate to get inside and be alone with my thoughts. I take off my slimy shoes. Looking around, I feel as though I need a shower before I try to walk down the pristine hallway. I study my feet and check there's no juice remnants, I don't want to stain the beautiful cream carpets, Jake would be so pissed.

I pad around the house, my house. It's so strange, the house is beautifully furnished, clearly every room has been well thought through and executed but I would never have guessed that this was *my* house. Even the Christmas decorations are very tasteful, a far cry from the old tatt that I usually put around the house. It might be old but it is sentimental, a lot of my decorations belonged to my Granny. I wonder where they all are? Do I still have them? I do love Christmas, normally. Clearly, I have much better taste in this new world.

My usual two-bed semi is choc-a-block with knick-knacks and colour whereas this beautiful six-bedroomed house is very minimalist, it gives the effect of looking very clean and tidy. The colour in the hallway is probably the most daring in the whole house and that's saying something. I go into the second living room and in there I find another bunch of flowers on the coffee table. I reach for the card.

L, the driver will pick you up at 8. Can't wait to see you. Your darling husband. Xxx

Wow, a second bunch of flowers. So far, in this crazy dream I have ascertained that I'm much better at my job. I'm three levels above where I currently am, my husband is better: note the flowers, and my house is amazing. What's not to like? I'm excited to see what will happen. I try to push down the memory of the meeting earlier. I can't get over how real this dream feels.

As my mind tries to compute what's happening, I begin to feel dizzy and exhausted again. I go and perch on the cream sofa. It looks brand new, a far cry from my much loved and ever so slightly stained, brown leather sofas. I hate to admit this is nowhere near as comfortable though. I glance at the ceiling, no cracks here. The whole room is beautiful.

In my new position I spy a metal framed picture. I need to find some clues for my new life or I'm going to be acting strangely to everyone around me and I want to make the most of this. I pick the frame up, feeling the weight in my hands lets me know this is an expensive frame.

I blink several times at the image, trying to focus on it. This isn't right. It's me on my wedding day, same dress, although my hair and make-up are different but the main thing that jumps out at me is the groom. It's not Jake in his soft grey suit anymore. The photograph is a lot more formal than the one we have in our house. No, this one is different. The groom stands to attention in a perfectly fitted black suit, tie and crisp shirt. He likes his suits like that, slim fit. I can feel myself start to hyperventilate at the memory of the kiss a few hours earlier, but in a completely different world.

I close my eyes, trying to bring myself to my happy place but now that place is filled with confusion. I feel so tired, I close my eyes and suddenly I'm slipping away, as I go all I can picture is *him* in that suit.

I married him?

Dom.

Chapter 7

Seven years earlier

'Right, you've been here for long enough, Lena. We need to keep getting you ready.' Jeanie sighs, offering me her arm to get up.

I shake my head enjoying the cold air and close my eyes, breathing in the scent of flowers. I could sit out here all day. It's beautiful, even if it is a bit chilly.

'It was all getting a bit much and busy in there,' I say, pointing back to the house. 'We've still got three hours; do I really need to be back in there now?' I whine, knowing full well Jeanie isn't having any of it.

'Well only if you want your hair and dress on in time.' She shrugs. 'Do you want to get married in a dressing gown, slippers and rollers?' She counts them off on her fingers, ready to argue with me further if needed. My parents' garden makes me feel calm and that's what I need right now. The butterflies rise up in my stomach and I think I might be sick.

'Fine, just give me fifteen minutes please,' I beg. 'Then I'll be the model bride. I just want to sit here and relax, just for a second.' I smile sweetly, hoping she won't pursue it any further.

I can see Jeanie considering her options, finally going for the path of least resistance. 'Fine, fifteen minutes but then you have to be back up in the room. No more breaks. I'll go and get *my* hair done now instead so the hairdresser can keep to time. Want me to send anyone down?' she asks, eyeing me almost suspiciously.

'No, no, you go. I just need a minute to myself then the rest of the day I'll be surrounded by people.'

'Okay, I'll just get your coat though, so you don't get too cold. You don't want your something blue to be you.' Jeanie laughs at her own joke and turns back to the house.

'No don't bother, it's actually nice to cool down.'

Jeanie looks at me as though I'm crazy but doesn't say anything.

I physically relax, trying to focus on the trees speckled with snow surrounding me, instead of the monumental day ahead.

We've not been together long, nine months is quick to get married, or so I'm reminded every time someone asks for the details. But when you know, you know, right? Then why am I sitting here feeling the panic rise in my chest? I close my eyes and try to calm myself. I'm doing the right thing. Jake and I are perfect for each other. I sit here with my thoughts, concentrating on making my breathing even. I love him. There's no question. Everyone gets cold feet. Don't they?

I hear a rustling, rousing me from my breathing exercises. Someone else is in the garden, has it been fifteen minutes already? No, it's probably Dad hiding away from all the action. He's been like a lost puppy this morning, the only man in the house.

'Dad?' I call out tentatively.

'No one has ever called me *that* before.' Dom chuckles as he emerges from the bushes. 'At least not in that way.' He smiles, raising his eyebrows at his joke. 'What are you doing out here anyway? It's freezing. Shouldn't you be getting ready?' He motions to my dressing gown and hair rollers, an amused look on his face.

Seeing his familiar face brings an instant smile to my lips, Dom's always been so easy to be around. I just wish Jake and Dom got along better but I can see they're very different.

'Yes, but I'm allowed to have a minute to myself. What are you doing out here?' I go on the offensive, tired of explaining myself.

'Came to see my wonderful neighbour, on her special day. I wanted to see how it was all going. Mum's been preparing the cake and clucking around our house all morning. She said to tell you it's looking good and she'll take it over to the barn soon.' Dom rolls his eyes. I bet his Mum has been talking about it non-stop, she was thrilled when we asked her to do the cake and she's kept me updated every step of the way since.

'Thanks,' I murmur flatly. I'm pleased. I really am, but I just need a minute to myself.

Dom nods knowingly, the smile disappearing from his lips. 'Cold feet?' he asks, taking his jacket off and popping it over my shoulders.

I shake my head but I don't really know the answer to that. Maybe it is cold feet? Or maybe it's everyone else's opinions getting into my head? I'm tired of it all, planning a wedding has taken all my energy, now I'm drained.

Dom feels like the last person I should be discussing this with.

'It's just all happened so fast,' I say quietly, hoping he won't try to delve any further. Jake is the love of my life. I know he is. I think. I suddenly feel the urge to cry but I hold back, unwilling to go through another hour of make-up.

Dom sits down on the bench next to me, appraising me. He slowly places his hand on mine, a tingle runs up my back. 'You don't have to go through with it, you know,' he says softly. 'Nobody would judge you.'

I look at him bewildered and snatch my hand away. What the hell? I love Jake, everyone gets cold feet on their wedding day, it's just nerves. It's totally normal. How can I not be nervous when everyone has been so adamant that we've rushed into this, but I know he's a good man. I know he's the man for me. It's just the thought of all the eyes on me all day. If it was just me and him it would be fine. I'm sure. I think.

He doesn't say anything but looks at me intensely and I see his hand edge nearer to mine again. At the last minute I see him decide against trying to take my hand. Instead he moves his body so he's facing me full on.

'Don't marry him,' he says it so quietly I could pretend that I've misheard.

I look at him searching his face, my mouth popping open. Is he serious?

Dom clears his throat and finds his voice. 'Marry me,' he says with a soft sincerity that I don't often hear from him.

Those two small words have taken the wind right out of me. I search his face for the joke, the laughter, the just kidding, but it doesn't come. Why now?

∞ ∞ ∞

Dom moved in next door over the summer holidays when he was just thirteen. My friends and I spent the summer spying on him from the windows of my house and reporting back to each other. We all thought he was so *hot* with his sandy blonde hair and cheeky, boyish face. I think you'd be hard pushed to find someone who didn't fancy him. Even the girls in the year above swooned over him.

When school started, who should join my tutor group but Dom. It felt like fate. I lusted after him for the rest of our years at school and although we became good friends nothing ever happened. I thought it would once. But I thought all that was in my imagination and now he's sitting here asking me to marry him. On my wedding day!

My head is swimming. I go to stand up and nearly pass out, my legs have turned to jelly. Dom turns to me and tries to grab my hand again but I pull it away. I look at him in disgust. Now? He chooses now? I'm furious.

Just then I hear the clip clop of shoes and a harassed looking Jeanie appears. She takes in the scene as Dom hurriedly drops his hand away. Jeanie looks between us, her lips pursed, but doesn't acknowledge the situation.

'Hair's ready for you. Come on,' she says, taking my arm and leading me away.

I don't dare say a word. I don't dare look back but I kind of want to.

I love Jake. I'm making the right choice. Aren't I?

Chapter 8

I open my eyes and peer cautiously around. I expected to be back in bed next to Jake, him softly snoring, but I'm still in that house. Dom's house. *Mine* and Dom's house. In this strange dream I must have decided to marry Dom.

I put my head between my legs and start to breathe, concentrating hard to stop myself hyperventilating again. I resign myself to the fact that either I've gone completely crazy or this is some wild dream. Either way, I might as well have some fun with it and see what my life could have been like. Now if I could only get myself under control. Although that has never been easy for me. The thoughts start to rise up again and I push them aside.

Already I see that if I had married Dom I would have done better in my career. Perhaps I did one of the qualifications through work. I probably went straight into working there after we were married, instead of aimlessly searching for the right career for me. Look what I could have achieved. I must have worked hard to get to the level I'm at. I've never really thought of this job as my career, something I'd do forever, but I never really thought of any of my jobs as something I'd do forever. Not in my real life, anyway. From working in shops, cafes and bars to various office settings, nothing has ever really sung to me. I've been okay at everything but not outstanding at any one thing.

I stand up and begin to pace around the room, trying to quieten my mind. Reminding myself it's just a dream, but I don't normally have dreams like this. What should I do now? I'm assuming that the time frame is the same but I don't really know. I turn on the telly desperate to find the date somewhere, anywhere. I pull up the TV guide and sure enough the date is the same, so seven years have passed and here I have married Dom instead of Jake. I wonder what happened to Jake? I feel kind of excited at the thought of Dom. If I kiss him now it's not so wrong. I'm not cheating on my husband. He *is* my husband.

I pad upstairs, re-searching the rooms. I'm not really sure what I'm looking for; I'll know when I see it. I feel restless and exhausted all at once. This new life is strange. I go into my bedroom and appraise myself in the full-length mirror. I'm horrified to see two large sweat patches under my armpits, the soft silk shirt has not hidden anything and on my sleeve is a big red smudge, presumably from when I wiped my top lip. I think back over the presentation and cringe at my ineptitude. God that was humiliating, but this is a dream so does it really matter? I take off my clothes looking at the expensive labels as I go. I could never afford any of this in real life, Jake would be so pissed if I spent this much money on clothes. They certainly feel like good quality though.

My hair is a bit messy from the sweat but it still looks better than when I did it this morning – in my real life. I appraise myself in my underwear. The extra layer around my middle has completely gone. I've never looked so thin in my life. I look amazing. Toned and tanned, a lot better suited to the well-turned-out Dom.

I decide to take a shower and find a beautiful en-suite with a huge roll top bath tub, his and hers sinks, a shower and toilet. It's beautifully tiled and finished, very modern, the towels are bright white and not a dangling thread in sight. I think to my threadbare blue towels at home, they could really do with replacing. I decide to take a bath, and it's every bit as luxurious and wonderful as I imagined. It's as though I'm staying in a fancy hotel rather than my own home. After forty-five minutes I climb out of the bath and wrap myself in the fluffiest bathrobe I've ever worn. It's amazing, I feel so relaxed.

I pad back into the bedroom and look around the room for my clothes, it's a huge but fairly plain room with a super-sized bed, mirror and a huge dressing table but no wardrobes, then I spot a door over in the corner. I wonder over and gasp, it's a massive walk-in wardrobe full of mine and Dom's clothes. I feel like a celebrity, it's almost bigger than my real bedroom.

I swoon over the expensive clothes, shoes and handbags. It takes me a while to find something to wear that is more comfortable and casual. A soft grey loungewear set. There are lots of dresses, underwear and swimming bikinis, well, if you look like this you might as well show it off, I suppose. I touch the expensive fabrics, marvelling at what could have been mine.

Looking around the house, I find another even larger bathroom, this one has a jet bath in it. I smile to myself, excited at the prospect of trying that out. The bedrooms are all beautifully decorated with a cream base and accents of different colours in each room. It's clear, as I look around, that it's only me and Dom who live here and I can't help but feel a little sad about that.

Suddenly an idea hits me. I rush back downstairs to find the soft leather handbag I brought home from work. Far smaller than the bag I usually take in. Perhaps this will tell me more about this new me. Except of course the obvious, I think smugly. I'm now extremely successful and married to a rich, gorgeous man who clearly still loves me, even after seven years. Just look at those beautiful flowers. I think bitterly of Jake not even remembering our anniversary. The contents of the bag are stark in comparison to the usual rubbish contained in my handbags.

I find an expensive looking purse; I scour the meagre contents. Some cash and cards but nothing overly exciting or telling. And a phone. Jackpot. Surely this will hold some clues? But it's passworded. I try my usual password, Spence200, but then I remember Spence isn't my dog anymore. I kind of miss his soft presence. Now what could my password be here?

As I sit there aimlessly tapping various passwords, a ginger tabby cat stalks into the room. I have a cat? I recoil, I've never been a cat person. It's not really that I dislike them, but I always saw myself as a dog person. Added to that, Jake came with his own dog and it's not surprising I never considered a cat. But a lot is different here.

On seeing me the cat pads closer. I can see a pretty, cream collar with a heart tag on it. It stands to reason that if my password is my dog's name in real life, perhaps the cat holds the key here. I hesitantly walk towards the cat who has jumped up onto the opposite sofa and is preening herself. I just need to have a quick look at that tag. The cat looks happy to see me at first purring but as I get closer, I see that something is amiss. She suddenly stands up on the seat flattening her ears and hissing at me. Perhaps she knows I'm an imposter? Or perhaps she's a really horrible cat? But I need that password so I edge closer.

I try to stay calm.

'Nice kitty, I just want to look at your name tag. Then I'll leave you alone,' I say in a calming voice. I take another step, offering her a cautious smile which is met with further hissing and now spitting. I didn't know cats spat. I'm close enough to see the tag but there's nothing on this side. I slowly move my hand in closer, hoping the cat will calm down. I'm about to take my arm away when the cat jumps forward and latches on with her claws, bares her teeth and bites down hard. I can hear the cat purring as she attacks me. This horrible cat is loving it. Perhaps it's Dom's cat and that's why she doesn't like me. Or maybe she knows.

'Owww, oww, oww.' Surely this cat is called *Evil* because she seems to be happy about hurting me. With the cat still attached to my arm I complete my mission and manage to flip the tag over. Squealing the whole time. I hope Dom doesn't come home because this would look like quite the scene. Finally, the name is in view, she is called Ginger. I retract my arm, bloodied from the cat attack and Ginger jumps down and scampers off, hiding away from me. I hope I won't have to see her again. I certainly won't be *touching* Ginger ever again.

I go into the kitchen to clean up. After scouring the cupboards, I finally find some Germolene and clean my arm up, coating the long scratches and hope they stop stinging soon. As I search out the bin, I notice a cat bowl which I didn't register before, I suppose I wasn't looking for it. There on the front of the bowl is written the word 'Ginger'. Great.

Once back in the living room I tap Ginger200 into my phone and it comes to life. Hurray. I start to look through my messages but there's nothing overly exciting. Messages to and from Dom about when we'll each be home and if we're away. Messages to someone called Brad, I scan through, and they appear to be a lot about diet and exercise. How dull. I look for anything from my friends but there's nothing there. There's not much on the phone at all really.

I begin to peruse the photographs. There's some of Dom and me in various hot and sunny places. Wow it looks like we take a lot of holidays, my beach body is looking fab too. I smile to myself.

I keep scrolling, seeing photographs of me looking very glam at some kind of dinner, having cocktails with girls I don't recognise. I'm smiling and I look very happy in all of the photos. I'm intrigued and a bit excited but I can't help but wonder where Marnie and Jeanie are.

The images only start from a few months back so it stands to reason that this must be a new phone and perhaps we haven't seen each other much recently. That can happen sometimes. Jeanie has an incredibly, busy important job which means she's away travelling often and Marnie is busy with her ever expanding brood. I look through the phone numbers, sure enough they're both there.

Before I know what I'm doing I've pressed call on Jeanie's number. Perhaps she'll be able to help me? Tell me how this all happened? Or perhaps she'll think I'm crazy, but I feel the fear rise in my chest and talking to one of them might bring me back down right now. It rings and rings but she doesn't answer. I look at the time: 7pm, how did it get so late? Jeanie could be working late in the office or out. I try Marnie thinking there's a better chance she'll answer. Although that depends if the kids have gone to bed.

She picks up on the third ring sounding harassed and tired. 'Hello, Marnie speaking.'

'Hi Marnie, it's me,' I say, feeling myself relax at the sound of a familiar voice.

'Who?' she asks.

'Lena,' I say, wondering how long it may have been since we last saw each other.

'Oh, okay. Um how can I help?' She sounds unsure and confused. Then I hear a lot of screaming in the background. 'Sorry, actually I'm going to have to go, the kids are going mental.' I hear some muffled crying in the background and Marnie shouts. 'Stop biting your sister,' clearly holding the phone away from her mouth. Abruptly she ends the call.

Marnie sounded so unfamiliar. Perhaps she was just distracted by the kids. That must be it. I can't imagine a world where we wouldn't be best friends.

Chapter 9

I decide to go and get dressed, after all I'll be meeting Dom in just under an hour for our anniversary dinner. I'm nervous just thinking about it. Will Dom know, like Ginger, that I'm not me? The memory of our stolen kiss in the office surfaces and I begin to feel hot and bothered. It's okay, he's my husband here I tell myself but I can't help feeling disloyal to Jake. Jake doesn't care, I remind myself. My stomach lurches and I think I'm going to throw up.

I go into the en-suite and splash some cooling water on my face. I'm suddenly ravenous, no point in eating anything now so I head into the walk-in wardrobe and flick through the clothes, trying to decide how dressy to be is difficult. There's a mix of gowns and dresses. In the end I settle on a classic little black dress which falls to the knee and with full sleeves to cover the cat scratches. It's understated but classic. I hope it's just right. I re-do my make-up and marvel at the ornate dark wood dressing table. This piece would never even fit in my bedroom. The drawers are full and organised. Even though I know this is all mine it doesn't feel like me. So tidy and organised. My house with Jake isn't a mess but it is cosy and colourful. It's such a stark contrast.

The car arrives sharply at eight and I'm excited to see where Dom's taking me. I peer through the windows trying to work out where in Twinton we are. Do I know this area? As we round a bend, I begin to recognise the look of the other houses, smaller than mine but still beautiful. It occurs to me there's only one area that looks like this and it must mean Marnie lives nearby.

∞ ∞ ∞

I arrive at the fanciest restaurant in town, Starletts. It's lit up with Christmas magic, twinkling fairy lights adorn the windows and I can't help but feel excited. I've never been here but everyone has heard of it. You only go if it's a real treat, and you have plenty of money to spare. Dom probably had to book this months in advance to get this date. It's gorgeous. I'm glad I dressed up but I probably could have gone even further. I walk in, unsure where I'm meeting him or what to call myself? Would I have taken his surname? I hover next to the sign which says wait here to be seated, fiddling with my dress and feeling nervous. I need a drink.

Finally, a waiter approaches. 'Hello Lena, usual table? Come straight this way,' he says.

I mumble a yes and follow him as he leads me through the bar and into the main restaurant. As we reach the back, I see him. It seems odd, the last time I saw him I was running out of his office and now I'm married to him. His eyes light up and it's clear he's happy to see me. When did Jake last look at me like that? The butterflies start to buzz around in my stomach, it feels like a first date for me, but it isn't for him. He looks so handsome in another of his expensive suits, his sandy hair has darkened with time but he still has the same cheeky grin. He stands as I approach the table. Coming straight over to me, arms wide.

'Happy anniversary, darling. You look beautiful,' he says, planting a kiss on my cheek. My face reddens at the familiarity but I enjoy the compliment and attention. It's so far removed from what I get with Jake right now. I could walk around naked and he wouldn't bat an eyelid. The waiter pulls out my chair and leaves us alone, informing us that someone will be by swiftly to take our order.

'How has your day been?' Dom asks, looking deep into my eyes. It feels weird to think of him as my husband. Of this being our everyday. Although I don't agree with Eli's assessment of him as an international playboy, I did always think it would take a lot for him to settle down. It was one of the reasons I didn't want to be with him, but looking at him now, asking about me, caring about me, I see how wrong I was.

'Um, good,' I start, unsure how to answer but wanting to make an effort. 'I wasn't feeling too well earlier, so I left early for the day but feeling much better now.' The rumour mill would have been spinning this afternoon, I don't doubt that even in this new world Dom probably already knows. I wonder if he knows about my presentation with Pearson and Sons.

'Fran said, she said you weren't acing like yourself. I'm glad you're feeling better.' He reaches across the table and squeezes my hand. Such a small and intimate gesture. If he does know about the meeting he's not letting on and I'm grateful, I don't want to dissect that again.

'How's your day been?' I ask, wondering if he was in the office and I just didn't see him or if he was in

London.

'The trains were a nightmare today but thank God, I made it back in time.' He smiles. 'Had to come straight to the restaurant though.'

'You didn't even get changed for me?' I tease, enjoying our new ease with each other. Normally it's all about business, well except when he kissed me in his office.

'Right,' Dom says, changing tack. 'Shall we have the usual or do you fancy looking at the menu?'

I've not eaten anything all day and the thought of food makes my stomach growl. I'm not sure what my usual is here. At home I'm most likely to order a pasta dish. I've not been here before so I'm keen to look over the menu.

'I'll have a look at the menu, I think. I'm ravenous,' I say. We both quietly contemplate our menus. All the dishes sound amazing. I wonder what my usual is? I really fancy a steak and I bet this place cooks them perfectly.

Dom looks up, 'I'm going to have my usual steak. Are you going to have the salad?'

Oh, so that's my usual, I try to hide my disappointment. Taut stomach explained but I don't want to waste my appetite on a salad. I don't think it'll fill me up and anyway a steak is full of iron, that's good for you. It's a special occasion.

'As it's a special occasion, I think I might have a steak too.' I smile. Dom physically baulks. This is obviously out of character for me.

'I know I don't normally have one,' I say holding up my perfectly manicured hand. 'But it sounds so good tonight, so why not?' I shrug my shoulders.

'I'm just surprised, that's all,' Dom flusters. 'I mean,

I didn't know you'd stopped being a vegetarian? What's it been? Five years since you ate meat? Are you feeling okay?'

Shit. What do I say to that? I'm a vegetarian? I'm learning a lot about myself. So, I either eat the meat and then I'm not a vegetarian, but everyone will watch whatever I'm eating and think I'm weird for suddenly stopping or I find a way out of this.

My mouth hangs open as I'm not entirely sure what to say. I begin to laugh. 'I'm only joking.' I look up at him and his expression changes and he begins to laugh too. 'See I can still get you, even after seven years.'

'Salad then?' he asks, smiling at my terrible *joke*.

'What else would I order?' I say, wishing I could have a steak.

When my salad comes, I have to admit it is rather delicious. Something about a very expensive restaurant means that even the salads are a bit more exciting. That doesn't mean to say that Dom's steak doesn't look more appetising. I wolf mine down in no time at all, helping myself to lots of bread and butter whilst Dom finishes up. I also take a large gulp of the champagne but even though it's expensive it tastes horrible. Is it corked? I swish it around in my mouth wishing I could spit it back out. I resolve to stick to the large jug of fresh iced water on the table instead.

'Hungry today, aye?' Dom says, his eyes twinkling with laughter.

'Oh yes, I didn't have lunch,' I explain, feeling my face flush. I'm not doing well at pretending to be me.

'Don't overdo it, isn't Brad coming in the morning?' he asks.

Who the hell is Brad? I think back to earlier and my phone messages, something about fitness and diet.

Maybe he's my nutritionist or a personal trainer. I can't think of anything worse than going for a run right now. I wonder idly if I can feign illness again but I've just convinced Dom I'm feeling much better.

'Um yes, I think so,' I say, noncommittally, hoping he doesn't ask more questions about someone I've never met.

'Can you believe it's almost been seven wonderful years together? Sorry we can't celebrate next week; these clients are relentless. I wish I could change it, but this is lovely isn't it?'

It stands to reason our wedding anniversary isn't the same as mine and Jake's, but it appears we didn't waste much time. I wonder if we eloped, I wonder if we had our family there or if it was just us?

'Yes, this is lovely. I know, I can't believe it.' I really can't. 'It was a beautiful wedding,' I say smiling warmly. Reminding myself he is my husband now and I'm trying to embrace that. I can't help but think back to Jake and wonder what happened to him that day. If this is my reality, what is his? Has he found someone else? Is he happy?

He chuckles. 'Yes, as beautiful as a Vegas wedding can be. That chapel was cute, but I never envisioned getting married by Elvis. We could do it again you know. Renew our vows on our tenth wedding anniversary. Invite all our family and friends.' He looks excited. I can't imagine Jake wanting to marry me once now, let alone twice. We're so disconnected. Whereas here's Dom, after seven years he's still trying. He's cleanly shaven and beautifully dressed, taking me out to a fancy restaurant, wining and dining me and practically asking me to marry him again. I may have made the wrong decision the first time but I won't waste this second chance.

'That would be amazing,' I say. 'I bet everyone was so annoyed we eloped without them.' I try to imagine what everyone's reactions were, they may have been annoyed at first but surely, they all came round?

'I don't think we should talk about all that, do you, darling? Let's focus on us, doesn't matter what happened.' He waves his hand dismissively, topic closed.

He's piqued my curiosity now. I have a sinking feeling in my stomach and I try to centre myself to stop my mind from spiralling. My parents have always loved Dom, so I don't think they would have an issue with us being together. Unless it's the eloping part, but I don't see them holding a grudge, not for this long. Surely my friends would have supported me? But Marnie was so distant on the phone, but she was distracted by the kids, so that's not unusual. I want to push the point further but I don't want to ruin the night.

'You're right,' I say, unsure how to continue. I know practically nothing about our lives together. I open my mouth to ask more questions but stop myself. I should know about my own life, if I keep asking questions, he's going to think I'm crazy. It's not as though I could tell him that in another universe I married Jake but I'm not happy and now I'm here married to him, Dom, evidently happier and not regretting the decision I made.

We sit quietly and continue with our meals. I begin to slowly butter another piece of bread. Lost in my thoughts, I can't help but compare my two lives. This life certainly feels like the better life. I'm fitter, more successful and my husband makes an effort with me, and still loves me.

I had a crush on Dom for such a long time and buried those feelings deep, sure that he would never choose me. When he proposed on my wedding day, I thought he was crazy and not really serious but look at where I could have been. Isn't this better? I was torn that day but my love for Jake won. Should I have let my lust for Dom win, look what it could have turned into. Well, in *this* world, has turned into.

I get through the rest of dinner with small talk and pretending I know what Dom is talking about. I'm only half paying attention because I'm trying to work out what has happened and who is still in my life. I'm also scared of slipping up again. On the drive back I catch Dom watching me.

'Are you alright? You've been quieter than usual,' Dom says, searching my face for clues. I love how much he cares.

'Just still feeling a little under the weather, I suppose.' I try to raise a smile but I'm exhausted from the whole day. My head feels heavy and I just want to go to sleep now. I sit back in the car and close my eyes, hoping we don't need to talk anymore.

'Poor darling,' Dom says, draping his arm around me. He turns to me and gives me the softest, sweetest kiss. I can feel his leg rubbing against mine and I'm taken back to our kiss in his office. This could have been my everyday. Butterflies dance inside me. I disentangle, not trusting myself.

I feel him start to stroke my arm and I can't help but feel disloyal to Jake. Even though Jake's not my husband here, I can't imagine having sex with Dom right now. Not on the first date, well *my* first date. I hope that's not what he's thinking is going to happen tonight.

I take Dom's hand and turn to him. 'I'm really not feeling great,' I say pointedly, hoping he catches the hint. 'I think I'm going to head straight to bed when we get in.'

'Okay,' Dom says, moving his hand away. I hope I haven't pissed him off but I don't have the energy to check. It's good to feel wanted in that way. For a change.

Once in I head straight to the bedroom and change back into the soft grey loungewear I had on earlier. I give Dom a quick kiss on the cheek and head off before he can try again, if he's mad, we can deal with it tomorrow. I'm grateful I've had a bit of time in the house earlier so I know the layout. I clamber into bed and fall asleep as soon as my head hits the pillow.

Chapter 10

I wake the next morning to a loud thumping sound. I shake my head to clear it and focus. Where is it coming from? Suddenly I realise it's the front door. I leap out of bed fumbling over myself to get my dressing gown on. I must look a right state. I wipe my drool covered cheek on my dressing gown. Yuck. As I pull open the door I try to smooth down my hair and not imagine the state my face must be in. Did I even take my make-up off last night? I probably look like a panda bear.

'Hello?' I say as I'm greeted by a tall, muscly man with a shaved head and piercing blue eyes. He's standing straight and to attention, he looks like he could be in the army by the way he's holding himself.

He looks me up and down and purses his lips, clearly not impressed. What's going on?

'Wake you, did I? I've been standing out here for ten minutes. Everything alright? Why are you not ready for our session?' he asks.

Session? I really take in the muscular Adonis now; he's dressed in shorts and a fitted t-shirt which is clearly made for working out. He must be Brad; didn't Dom say something about him coming over?

'Yes, sorry. I wasn't feeling well yesterday and I

must've overslept. I'll go and get ready.' I let Brad in and tell him to help himself to anything in the kitchen, although really, I have no idea what's there. I'm also slightly terrified at the thought of having to do a full workout with this man. He obviously works out daily and is super fit. I haven't done a full workout in years.

I joined the gym last January but I got sick of how busy it was and resolved to go back once all the "New Year's resolution" joiners disappeared, but of course I was one myself so I never went back. Too ashamed to cancel the membership I let the gym take my money for the next six months before I cancelled it.

Back upstairs I find my gym gear and pull on figure-hugging yoga pants and a top which shows my mid-drift. This a far cry from my usual oversized joggers and t-shirt, but looking at myself in the mirror I look amazing. I feel a little bloated from all the bread I ate last night but you can't even see it. I can see why Dom mentioned it now. I hope I'm able to keep up with Brad. I can feel butterflies dancing around in my stomach at the thought. I find my watch and notice the time is 6.45am, wow we start early, this is crazy and then I go to work? No wonder I'm so toned.

I totter down the stairs. Brad's drinking some kind of green juice he has made himself, and evidently me, from the cupboards.

'You don't have to drink this now, but you could have it later on.' Brad smiles, his face really lights up and his military persona disappears. I bet Brad can be really good fun when he wants to be.

'Okay, we'll start with the usual 5k, but I don't think we'll be able to fit everything in the session now,' he says, back to business. 'I have another client after you. Do you think you could do the weights and stretches yourself today? Your next session is booked in Thursday, isn't it?' He eyes me, he knows full well that's when it's booked in but he's making sure I don't pull this trick again.

'Yes, Thursday. Okay, great,' I say but I'm considering feigning illness again. Brad doesn't look like the type to put up with me stopping every ten minutes. How long does it take to run 5km? Thirty minutes? Forty-five minutes? I consider asking but if he says twenty minutes I might pass out from the thought. Is he expecting a sprint?

The sky is clear and there's been a frost overnight, I'm already regretting my choice of outfit. Why didn't I wear a jumper? We stretch ourselves out in the front garden, the trees surrounding the house keep it quite private and secluded. I imagine doing this at home with Jake, our front garden is merely gravel and we live on quite a busy road; I would look beyond ridiculous.

Finally stretched we begin to run, as I move my legs I begin to get into a rhythm and I'm surprised at how easy the run is for me. No puffing and panting, but controlled breathing. I keep up with Brad relatively easily and I even find myself quite enjoying it. My body warms up and I'm glad I don't have more clothes on, weighing me down. I begin to wonder why I let myself go so much in my real life and as the endorphins kick in, I begin to feel really great. I marvel at how much difference it makes to my usually anxious mind. The worries about heading back to the office after yesterday's faux pas have lifted a little.

As we get back to the house Brad checks his watch.

'Hmm two minutes over our usual pace, not great,' he says, bursting my bubble. 'How's your eating been going?'

'Um pretty good, it was my anniversary dinner last night so…' I let the words hang in the air while Brad gives me a stern look. Right, I should have just lied.

'Okay well, make sure you drink that juice I made you and get back on it,' Brad instructs. 'On Thursday I don't have any clients after so we could do a double session? It's important over the Christmas period to not let your standards drop.'

We stretch out again in the front garden and he gets me to do a few strength exercises before he suddenly looks at his watch.

'Crap,' he mutters under his breath.

'Something wrong?' I ask innocently.

'I better go or I'm going to be late for my next session. Because we started late, I didn't realise the time.' He gestures wildly. I can sense his annoyance and I note to myself that I better be on time Thursday or I'll never hear the end of it.

With that Brad leans in and plants a kiss on my cheek. It seems a bit weird for a personal training session but I've probably been working out with him for years so maybe this is normal?

'Okay, thanks,' I say trying to ignore the uneasy feeling in my stomach. 'I'll let you know about the double session.'

'I could make it really fun,' he says raising his eyebrows. I'm not sure I'm buying the fun that he's selling. I smile tightly and turn, heading back into the house. Brad jogs off, presumably to his next job. What was that all about?

∞ ∞ ∞

Back in the house I go up and take a shower. I check

the clock, 7.45am. I can't help but marvel, I've already done a workout but normally I'd be switching off the snooze button and forcing myself out of bed. I go into my huge walk-in wardrobe and pick out a smart outfit for my first full day as a big boss, although no one knows it's my first day. I'm nervous, can I pull it off?

I stroll down the stairs and that's when it occurs to me that Dom isn't here and he wasn't here when I woke up. How early does he head off? Is he having a PT session too? At the bottom of the stairs on the side table is a fresh bunch of flowers, some chocolates and a card. As I get closer I can see it's addressed to me. I open it hastily.

L, sorry to leave before you're up. I've got a few big meetings in London, set up last minute. I'll be back on Christmas Eve. I love you. D xx

I can't help but feel both disappointed and relieved. It's hard pretending I know about our lives but I was looking forward to spending more time together and seeing what it's like to be married to him. Why didn't he mention it last night? Perhaps it was booked after I went to bed, I know he tends to work flat out and sometimes late into the night. Eli may well think he's a playboy but there's no denying his work ethic, even Eli admits Dom's a hard worker.

I grab my bag and head out to drive to work. Once on the driveway I remember Fran gave me a lift home so whatever my car is it's at work. What do I do now?

Chapter 11

I frantically search my purse and then house for some cash so I can order myself a taxi. It's too far away to walk to work, I imagine tottering in my high, designer heels. Anyway, it's cold and rain is forecast. I don't want to turn up looking like a drowned rat, especially after yesterday. What am I going to do now? Then I remember the little shop around the corner from Marnie's has a cashpoint. Brilliant I'll go and get some cash there and then head to work.

I wrap up warm, I won't be jogging this time so I know I'll feel it a lot more. It takes me a bit of wandering around to finally find Marnie's house and then onto the corner shop. I just hope I don't get lost on the way home. The streets are like a maze and all the roads and houses look similar, that is apart from my house and the ones close by. I try to take in the Christmas decorations and record in my mind which ones have trees in the window as a kind of map back to my house, just follow the Christmas trees.

Once at the shop I rummage in my bag and find my purse. I queue up and finally at the cashpoint I find myself sighing with relief but all too soon when I take out my bankcard and see my name. Mrs L Clarke. Shit.

So I did take his name.

I hadn't even thought but clearly my pin won't be the same. Idly I tap in my normal pin. Nope. I try every other card and various other numbers I can think of. There's a bit of a queue forming behind me and I can feel the panic beginning to build in my chest, my hands are sweaty and clumsy and I find myself fumbling around and dropping my cards. The calming effect of the exercise long forgotten.

I hear a little voice behind me. 'Mummy, what's that lady doing? Why are all her cards on the floor? She's been there for agggggggeeeeeesssss. I'm bored and I want some sweets. Is it our turn now?' Whilst she talks, I can hear some desperate shushing but it's in vain, this little girl doesn't care.

I hear her mother speak. 'Shhh, darling, we need to wait for our turn. She's using the machine and during her turn she can take as long as she needs.' Although her words are kind, she's clearly embarrassed and exasperated. I keep my face forward not daring to glance at them while I finish off. Finally, I admit defeat. I don't know my pin, so I can't get any money.

I think desperately, what are my options now? Maybe, I can try my luck in the shop, get some cashback. I wander in thinking this is a brilliant plan. It's only a very small shop and as I walk down the aisles, I pick up a few little pieces. Some chocolate and a drink. I bet this body hasn't had chocolate in a while, Brad will be sickened. As I join the queue, I hear the familiar voice of the little girl. 'Mummy, can I have some sweets? Are we nearly done? I'm cold and hungry.' Typical child always thinking of their tummy.

'No,' replies the mum. 'We're going home soon and you can have a snack there. You don't need any sweets we just came out for milk and eggs and we'll make a cake this afternoon.' I can hear the little girl huffing. I'm amused because she really reminds me of my little goddaughter, Penny, so demanding at three, almost four and she'll make sure you know it.

As they join the queue behind me, I glance back and that's when I see that the reason she reminds me of Penny, is because it *is* Penny. Marnie is looking suitably harassed and I'd assume that in that buggy she's pushing sits Dana, but she's turned towards Marnie. I can hear Dana fussing and Marnie is clearly trying to soothe her and keep her quiet. I think of all our conversations about how embarrassed Marnie gets when the kids cause a scene, she's clearly getting more and more stressed the longer she waits.

As Penny locks eyes with me, she starts to pull at Marnie's clothes to get her attention. 'Mummy, Mummy,' she says loudly. 'Look it's that woman,' she says, clearly pointing at me. 'I think I've seen her before.'

Marnie looks up horrified by her oldest daughter's outburst and recognises me for the first time. 'Oh, hello, Lena. I'm so sorry.' She looks towards Penny now. 'That's enough, Penny.'

'But Mummy I've seen her before,' she whines, as if that'll make it all okay. It dawns on me that Penny doesn't know me here. In the normal world she'd be all kisses and cuddles, demanding I pick her up although she's too big for that really and telling me about her favourite dinosaurs, *it's a Argentinasaurus don't you know, they're the biggest?*

I can't help but feel sad. I'm a stranger to her here, in this wonderful dream I have Dom but I don't have one of my best friends.

'Yes darling, we saw Lena outside at the cashpoint remember?' Marnie soothes, trying to quieten Penny down, but Penny's getting irate. Yes, I was the woman dropping my cards I think to myself but I don't say anything. No point making it more uncomfortable for Marnie.

'No, Mummy. That's not where *I* saw her. Well I did but I've seen her before.' She really begins to scrutinise me now. Does she know? Is it like with Ginger? Can she feel that somewhere else, we know each other? Children and animals are more in tune with things like this, or so they say.

'It's okay,' I say to Marnie. 'I've not seen you in a long time, how long's it been?' I ask, almost afraid to hear the answer. How long have I gone without being a part of her life? Obviously, it's been more than four years, has it been even longer than that? How sad that we drifted apart. I can't imagine my life without Marnie and her adorable children.

Marnie gives me a weird look. She doesn't look particularly interested, before she has the chance to answer Penny pipes up, 'I've got it Mummy. She lives in the bin.' Penny turns to me, a look of triumph on her face, she's worked it out and she's proud to let everyone know. 'The bin, the bin. She lives in the biiiiinnnnnnn.' She starts to sing at the top of her voice, pointing at me as she does. Marnie looks mortified. She bends down to Penny's level and in hushed tones, that everyone in the shop can still hear, tells her to stop it right now or she will not be watching any TV today or make a cake later. Penny abruptly stops, the threat is clearly enough, but she's not happy that Marnie isn't impressed with her discovery.

'But she does live in the bin, Mummy,' Penny

whinges to Marnie, putting her tiny arms on her hips. 'Remember you were cutting up photos for your album and *that lady,*' she says, thrusting her little fingers towards me, 'lives in the bin. You told me so, Mummy.' She crosses her arms triumphantly.

Marnie looks horrified and, as she looks at me, I can see the pity in her eyes. She puts her hand over her mouth, I don't think she knows what to say. What is there to say? Dana begins to wail and she busies herself dealing with her. I turn my head forward and try to shake off what I've just heard, but I can't help but feel the big, hot tears fill my eyes. Ouch. A three-year-old has just made me cry. I can't let them see.

Marnie and I have never had a big falling out, sure we've had little disagreements over the years. We've been friends since we were eight years old after all, we fought over Barbies and boys but I would never have imagined a big enough fight for us to stop being friends.

'Next,' calls the elderly man on the till. 'Next!' he calls again louder and I suddenly realise he's talking to me. I shake myself out of my pity stupor and approach the till, grateful to be away from Marnie and Penny.

I don't even look back; I don't want to hear about the bin lady anymore. Who am I in this world? Why would Marnie throw my pictures in the bin? Did we have a horrible falling out?

I place my items down and I almost forget to ask for cashback, my mind is so preoccupied with Marnie and Penny.

'Sorry love, we don't have enough cash for cashback at the moment. There's a cashpoint outside though.' He smiles, seemingly solving all my problems. Little does he know I don't know my PIN. I thank him all the same for the information and hover my card over the machine. Holding my breath and praying there will be no reason for me to tap in my PIN number. My stomach churns, I feel sick. I have to remind myself the cards are technically mine. This is my life, well kind of. I don't have anything to worry about it's not as though anyone's going to arrest me. I'll just tell them I've forgotten my PIN, if I have to.

But it's fine. I hurry out of the shop deliberately keeping my head down and away from Marnie. I want to ask her what went so terribly wrong that our friendship ended up in her bin but maybe ignorance is bliss. Was it my fault? Was it hers? I guess I'll never know.

∞ ∞ ∞

I head down a few dead ends, my Christmas tree map clearly wasn't good enough, but I manage to get back to the house. I'm relieved to be back "home" but I can't help but long for the cosiness of my real home, the clutter, the lived-in feel. This beautiful house suddenly feels less stylish and more stark and cold. I wish I could see Dom's handsome face, that would help. Perhaps he is what makes this place feel like home? I sit down on the plush sofa. Now what? I hesitate knowing what I need to do, I tap through my phone and press call.

Fran answers the call sounding more like her usual harassed self. 'Hello?' She's not one for pleasantries.

Suddenly I feel nervous. I start to tap my hand, lifting my finger up and down, up and down. Rhythmically soothing myself.

'Hello, sorry to bother you Fra…' I start but she cuts me off.

'Oh, I'm so sorry I didn't realise it was you.' Fran's tone becomes soft and friendlier. Perhaps she is my friend here. It brings me a bit of comfort to think I have someone, even if it's not someone I would have considered a friend normally. Perhaps now I'm the boss we're able to be friends. She was never good at that, everyone thought of her as a bit of an ice queen, separate from everyone else.

'No problem, Fran,' I say brightly. 'I know you must already be at work and I wouldn't ask but I'm completely stuck. I left my purse in my car which is at work. Is there any chance you could come and pick me up and bring me into work? Then I can pick up my car and purse and get myself home.'

'Oh, um.' I can hear the hesitation in her voice but I think she wants to help. 'I'm about to go into a meeting, you know with Mark, Gavin and John. It's important. *Especially* after yesterday.' With that comment my face flushes hot and I wince, I shake my head, I don't want to think about that again but the word 'Horning' plays in my mind on repeat. I cringe. 'I'll see what I can do though. Hold tight and I'll let you know.'

'Thank you so much,' I say. 'You're a life saver.' It suddenly dawns on me it's nearly 9.30am. 'Remind me, am I in this meeting? Do you need me?' I ask crossing my fingers she doesn't, as I'll really be no help anyway, as yesterday's performance can attest to.

'No, not at all, don't worry I can handle everything.'

Relieved I take myself into the kitchen and wolf down my chocolate bar, savouring the taste in my mouth. Ten minutes later I get a quick text to say a lift will be coming asap. I don't know why I didn't just ring Fran in the first place at least then I could have avoided the whole Marnie incident. I pace around the room and open the fridge for the fourth time hoping that something appetising has appeared, the chocolate didn't quite hit the spot. Instead I notice the green juice Brad left this morning. I take a quick sniff, and consider throwing it out but maybe it tastes better than it smells. I can't help but feel a bit guilty about the chocolate. Here I am perfectly toned and all I need to do is maintain it and I shove a chocolate bar straight in my mouth. I bet this new, glamorous me would never normally do that. She's a vegetarian, after all.

I pour the contents into a cup to keep it nice and cool and resolve to take it with me to work. Perhaps everyone's eyes on me will help me force it down my neck. It's good for me. Here I'm super healthy. Brad would be so pissed off if he knew about the chocolate bar, the least I can do is swallow down this putrid green gunk, surely that will cancel it out, won't it?

∞ ∞ ∞

Twenty minutes later there's a knock on the door. I pull it open to find Eli there and I'm happy to see a familiar face. It may be one that is a bit bitchy but we have an easy banter and I know he likes me really. That's just his way of showing it.

'Hello, took you long enough,' I say, theatrically rolling my eyes. Ready for a bit of back and forth.

I wait for his witty retort but it doesn't come. 'I'm so sorry, I came as quickly as I could,' he gushes, he seems worried. 'I left the office as soon as Fran asked, although it took me a while to find your house,' he admits. He looks almost nervous, who is this arse kisser? Is this how all the big bosses are treated. Well you know what they say; it's lonely at the top.

'It's fine, really. I was joking,' I say, not wanting to embarrass him further.

I climb into Eli's car and we drive to the office without speaking. There's a palpable atmosphere of tension in the car. Eli isn't the type to keep his snipes in so this must be killing him. I try to keep calm and stop myself from thinking about yesterday. Instead I focus on the houses, searching out trees in the windows, lit up, beautiful and Christmassy and enjoy the Christmas music on the car radio – *I Wish It Could be Christmas Every Day* is playing – which I suspect Eli has put on to prevent any further conversation. Oh well, it could be worse.

Perhaps this Christmas isn't going to be so bad, after all I have Dom. It couldn't be as bad as last Christmas anyway.

Chapter 12

When we reach Morgans, I head straight to my personal office. I debate pulling the blinds round but decide against it. I don't want anyone hyperventilating over a potential firing, although thinking about it, that mainly seemed to be me. I type in my password Ginger200. I know Fran is in a meeting, so I busy myself going through my emails and trying to work out what I should be doing.

I cringe at the thought of yesterday's presentation, remembering all their appalled faces. I should have been able to do that straight forward presentation, perhaps they were right about my promotion, but now I'm way above where I should be and I need to fake it till I make it, as they say. If I work hard, surely I can do this. Although the heaving in my chest suggests otherwise. I could do with another run right now. Look at me, thinking about exercise.

I sit still in my chair trying to calm the doubts, I close my eyes and lean back into the leather chair letting it take my full weight. I imagine my happy place again, this time in summer, green and warm, beautiful flowers everywhere. I can do this; I can do this. I start to repeat it over and over in my mind. At the end of the day this is a dream, a frightfully realistic and long dream, granted, but if I can't be fabulous here, where can I be?

With that in mind, I open the email from Mark at Pearson and Sons and see an extensive list below which Fran has typed up of our next steps. I quickly hit print and bring it over to my desk, I run my hand down the list. Now this I can get on board with. I love a good list and to my delight, I think I can do some of this.

I forward the email back to Fran and say I'll work on the first two bullet points, if she can do the others and could she pop into my office for a debrief on the meeting once it's finished. I feel empowered telling Fran what to do. Even though she seems more like the boss, even here, she's handling everything but that's just because I've been "ill" and isn't that what a good second does? I need to take control. I can be assertive; I can be confident. In your faces interview panel, I'll show you here in this dream. Where you'll never see it, I think ruefully.

Over the next hour I work hard and find myself completely immersed. I'm pleased with the work I've done and have checked against similar pieces and it seems in keeping, maybe even a good job I chastely admit to myself. Fran raps loudly on the door, despite her wallflower exterior there are still remnants of her loud, extroverted, boss-woman self.

'Hi, I was wondering if you're free for the debrief of the meeting?' she asks softly, back to wallflower I see.

'Yes, that would be great. I'm so sorry I didn't make it in time.' Although of course I'm not after yesterday. The thought of that presentation makes my stomach swirl again.

'Mark just wanted to go over everything with me. He was a little worried after um...' Fran looks awkwardly down, not usually one to mince her words, it's strange to be on the receiving end of this more considerate Fran. I can see that she's trying not to hurt my feelings, but my presentation, not knowing their names and generally looking like a crazy person has done some damage to the client's confidence in us. Crap.

'Okaaay,' I say, not really sure what to say after that. 'Well, I've been working on the first few bullet points we outlined. Are you happy to work on the rest like I suggested?' I take charge, reminding myself I can do this. I can be the boss. I am the boss.

Fran gives me a big smile. 'That's great,' she says brightly. 'Could you send it over to me and I'll make sure we send everything together. Keeps it tidy.'

I nod happily. I'm feeling pretty chuffed with myself. I tap out an email and send it over to Fran. 'I'll have the next part finished later today and I'll send that over to you too.' I return her bright smile, feeling pleased with myself.

Fran proceeds to fill me in on the meeting, which just appears to be a repeat of yesterday, albeit it without my awful non-presentation.

'Perhaps you could show Kian around the whole company this afternoon?'

'Kian?' I ask confused. Who's Kian?

'Yes, Kian our new manager. I know you haven't met him yet. He started yesterday, remember?'

'Ah yes, Kian. Sorry. In all the preparing for Christmas I'd completely forgotten.' I think back to Fran parading him around the office on his first day and it occurs to me that here, I am Kian's line manager.

'Of course,' Fran says kindly. 'So, is this afternoon okay?'

'Yes, that would be fine. I'll come out and introduce

myself once I've finished this.' I'm keen to get on and prove I'm not a complete waste of space.

It's nearly lunchtime and I've made great headway on the next bullet point; I should have everything completed by the end of the day. I'm beginning to feel quite good about it all. It's really not so hard. I never really saw this job as my calling but perhaps the work was just not challenging enough for me. I look down at my smart suit, my big beautiful ornate desk and I can't help but marvel at my success. Look at me. I'd never have imagined it. Look at what I could/can achieve. I almost feel like singing.

I look out into the office at all the worker bees, I was one of them and I worked my way up here. How did I do it, I muse. Did I do a university course in the evenings? Beavering away at home and work to make everything work? Did I learn on the job, working long hours, ensuring I understood something before moving onto the next thing? Maybe I'll never know but whatever I did, I worked hard for it. You don't get this kind of job overnight.

As I'm staring out at my old desk watching the dowdy version of Fran tap tapping at her computer and Eli slurping another huge smoothie, yuck, I see two elegant ladies enter the office. They're dressed to impress and would be more suited to a lifestyle magazine than the likes of this office. Surely, they don't work here? One has red hair that is tied into a tight chignon and the other has oodles of long blonde hair perfectly coiffed and styled into soft curls that cascade down her back.

I can't help but think they look exactly like the kind of girls that Dom used to parade around the office. Should I feel threatened? Tall, beautiful and very sure of themselves. Unfortunately, most of them, aside from their looks, didn't have a great deal going on and Dom would grow tired of them quickly and be onto the next. Hence Eli naming Dom an international playboy. I remind myself that Dom is with me now, I don't need to worry about these girls anymore, just look at our beautiful life together. I always thought he just needed to find the right girl; I never dreamed that would be me. Until now.

As I watch the long-legged beauties parade through the office, I can't help but notice each head turn in their direction. They're oblivious, so used to being watched they keep their focus straight ahead. If I didn't know any better, I could swear they're headed in my direction. Surely not? What would these knockouts want with me?

As I watch them it suddenly dawns on me that I recognise their faces but from where? It's not until they're standing outside my office that I realise. They are some of the glamourous ladies from the photos in my phone. It appears they *are* here to see me.

The pretty blonde peers through the door and gives it a quick tap before opening it seconds later, I don't suppose she's used to waiting for anything or anyone.

'Daaaarling,' she drawls, her pretty, blonde face lighting up as she sees me. All smiles and air kisses. 'Oh, look at you, you look busy.' She pushes her big bottom lip out. 'Are you ready for lunch?' She delves into her bag and produces a compact mirror, checking her perfect make-up, she gets out her lippy and proceeds to paint the same deep red on her lips. It looks no different when she's finished. I watch her in awe, not answering.

'So?' Redhead asks impatiently, hand on hips. 'Come on, our reservation.'

I glance at the clock on the back wall. Lunch? I've been working away so much it's already 1.30pm. I'd rather stay here and finish what I'm doing but my stomach gives an involuntary rumble. The thought of something more delicious than Brad's green smoothie in the fridge makes my mouth water. Must make sure I order from the vegetarian side of the menu this time though, I think, sadly.

'Um yes,' I say, what choice do I have? Girl's got to eat. 'It'll have to be a quick one though, I've got lots of work to do.' I smile sweetly.

They exchange a look and both burst into laughter as if I've just told the funniest joke they've ever heard. If they're this easily amused this lunch is going to be easy. Even if I don't know their names. Hopefully they'll say them at some point and I won't have to worry.

We head out into the office and I can feel all eyes on us, heads turning as we leave. As we head past Fran's desk, I inform her I'm out to lunch and will finish my work when I'm back. She nods and smiles but barely looks up from her desk, so engrossed in what she's doing.

∞ ∞ ∞

As we leave the office the girls are chattering about Christmas and what they're doing and what they've prepared. It occurs to me I have no idea what Dom and I are doing for Christmas. Is it a cosy one just the two of us? Is it with my parents or Dom's parents or both? Am I about to host a huge Christmas bash that I've neither prepared for, or had any idea about? I resolve to call Mum later and try to subtly find out what she's up to (if that's possible?) and try to make sure I'm ready.

Christmas for Jake and I is normally a huge family affair. We split the days over Christmas and boxing day between his family and mine, alternating Christmas each year. His mother uses every available opportunity to snipe at me about one thing or another and I end up drinking a copious amount of alcohol to deal with her. On Boxing Day in the evening, we see Jeanie and whoever she's seeing and Marnie, Mitch and the kids. Usually hosted by Marnie so she can get the kids into bed as soon as possible and have a few glasses of vino. It's something I look forward to every year and it feels odd that here I won't see them. I can't help but wonder where Jeanie is, I bet she's off on her travels. My stomach aches and I can't help but miss them. Although these glamour-pusses seem very nice, they're not my friends. Not the ones *I* know anyway.

'We're going to Greece to be with Gerald's family this year,' Blonde groans. 'I'm kind of looking forward to it, but I will miss you girls so much,' she says, popping her bottom lip out again, is that a thing now? Pouting at every opportunity?

'Well we're skiing, heading out tomorrow,' says Redhead a bit more business-like. Her eyes are a beautiful green and up close she's even more striking than I thought when she entered the office, she must be a model. 'A lovely white Christmas. I can't wait. I just wish this one here,' says Redhead, nudging me, 'was coming with us like we planned. Dom and his workaholic ways ruin *everything*. You should've come without him.' She rolls her eyes at me. Wow skiing, how glamourous. I wonder if I'm any good at it. I'm glad we're not skiing though. I don't think I could fake being able to ski when I've never been.

So, Dom and I are spending it together, butterflies start to swim in my stomach at the thought of Dom and me and Christmas. Even though here we're married it still feels like the early days of dating for me and I'm excited to get to know more about him and our life together. I bet he's so romantic, I wonder what he'll get me for Christmas. Last Christmas Jake got me a handful of perfumes, yes, a handful of perfumes. Lots of different tiny perfume bottles, you'd normally get something like that from boots in a pretty box but that's not how he presented it. Instead they were wrapped up loosely in a ball, it was bizarre. I wasn't entirely sure how to react, it's not all about the presents but a pair of earrings or a necklace wouldn't go amiss.

And let's not even think about my last birthday where he got me a pair of slippers. I'd gotten to the point where I didn't expect much but it still disappoints me that Jake could never think of anything to get me despite being married to me for so long.

'Well, you know Dom.' I shrug, hoping that this conveys whatever she wants to hear. Clearly, I can't bear to be away from him. We must have something nice planned. 'He's away on business at the moment but he'll be back tomorrow evening for our work Christmas Eve party.' I smile, glad I have something to tell them that I actually know.

We head down the high street and into one of the quirky bar/restaurants. The kind of place that I'd normally feel really out of place. I bet the vibe is quite different in the evening. It's all bright lights, and trendy seating of different types, a mismatch that somehow works and looks incredible. Even the waiters and waitresses look like they've stepped out of a style catalogue.

We sit down in one of the booths, Redhead and Blonde opposite me. The girls are chatting about the holidays they have planned for next year and I can't help but feel slightly awkward. I'm relieved when the waitress comes over, she's very young and hip and dressed in black.

As we sit there the waitress leans in with her hand held high, 'Hi,' she says. She's staring straight at me, greeting me; these places are so weird. I put my hand up too and give her an enthusiastic high five. Might as well get into the spirit of things.

I look around the table waiting for her to high five Blonde and Redhead but instead she continues to reach forward and picks up the menus next to me, flipping them over. She recovers well from the unexpected high five, smiling away but my friends are looking at me as though I'm crazy. What an idiot I am. I feel my face start to turn scarlet, this is so embarrassing. I breathe deeply; it's happened now so I might as well own it.

'That's how all the restaurants are doing it in France,' I say. I have no idea if that's true, and I hope they don't either.

Redhead starts to laugh. 'You're hilarious, Lena.'

After that the lunch isn't quite so awkward, I mean I couldn't really do anything more embarrassing. I even enjoy the girls' company. We order an expensive bottle of wine but it tastes awful to me, probably because I usually drink the cheap stuff. Not wanting to draw more attention to myself or harass the waitress any further I don't say anything. Instead, I stick mainly to the water on the table which is better anyway, as I've got lots of work to do after this.

I manage to order lunch without issue and I'm pleased I made the vegetarian mistake when I was with

Dom, I don't think they'd have found that joke very funny.

'Any New Year's resolutions Lena?' Blonde asks.

'Hmmm, not yet. What about you?' I ask.

'Same old, try to lose some weight she says looking down at her non-existent stomach.' I'm flabbergasted by this knockout saying that, it humanises her a bit more to me. I suppose everyone has their hang ups, even if they're completely unfounded. She'd have thought the other me an obese monster when really, I was just a bit overweight.

'Me too,' adds Redhead. 'Also, now that my work is taking off, I resolve to make sure I spend plenty of time with my good friends. I don't want to let work take over.' She gestures wildly, as though that could be the worst thing in the whole world but with three holidays already planned next year, I'm not sure how it could take over.

These girls are kind of sweet, it really seems I've not done too badly.

Lunch arrives and we all tuck in quietly, away with our own thoughts about the New Year. Christmas is such a reflective time and I can't help but think about my plans with Jake, our plan to do it all over again but we don't seem in the right place for it. Not now.

After wolfing down lunch and watching the others push their food around the plate, I glance at my watch: it's nearly 3.30pm. I've been out the office for 2 hours.

'I can't believe the time. I need to get back to the office.'

'Check you out, working so hard. Okay, lovely. We'll see you for New Year's, though right?' Redhead asks.

'Right.' I smile, quickly throwing a huge tip on the table and air kissing everyone, because that's what you do, right? I practically run back to the office. I hope Fran hasn't been waiting on my work for too long.

∞ ∞ ∞

When I get back it's nearly 4pm and I can't see Fran anywhere to apologise. I'll quickly get it done and then she can send everything over to Mark. I head into my office and sign in quickly checking my emails for anything urgent, I see an email to Mark from Fran. I scroll through and read it, thinking perhaps she's had to go home so will have said I'll send the last of it, but to my surprise all the work has been completed. Even the work which is half done on my computer. Fran must've done it. I feel dreadful, I download the document, she's collated it all into one. As I scroll through, I see the work that is supposed to be mine but it's not mine. Fran has redone everything. All of it. I've completely wasted my time.

Chapter 13

I can't believe that Fran has redone my work. I'm her boss. I don't know whether to call her out on it, but maybe she was just saving my arse. Perhaps this is some uncharacteristically poor work. Then I notice an email to me before the Mark email, just saying she was leaving for the day and she hoped I didn't mind she did the other piece and hoped I enjoyed my lunch with the girls. No mention of her redoing it, perhaps she didn't want to embarrass me. I feel like a fraud, so terrible at this job that Fran had to save me. Again.

I decide to pack up for the day and head home, it takes me a while to work out where my car is and a lot of pressing the buttons at various fancy cars before I locate my BMW. A top of the range BMW, and it's all mine.

I'm pleased to get home and be able to shut myself away. I run a hot bath in the main bathroom and think back over the events of the last few days, letting the jets wash away everything that has happened.

I can't help but feel nervous at the thought of Dom returning. At the thought of his name I look through my phone, he's sent me a text about how boring the meetings are and he wishes he was at home with me. I can't wait for Christmas. He's so sweet, always letting me know he's thinking of me; even though we're not in the same house I feel closer and more visible to him than I do Jake. Dom's such a hard worker, always at the London office meeting with important clients and furthering the business. I wonder if I ever go into London with him. Perhaps I'll ask him if I could come next time, make a weekend of it.

Dom's hardly been here all week which is such a contrast to Jake, he's always shuffling around the house. Over Christmas he's always there too, it's almost too much and annoying. I can't help but miss having the company but I understand what Dom is trying to do and it's important. I bet it's not always like this either, it's just because everyone's trying to finish things off before the Christmas break. When Dom comes back tomorrow evening, we can have lots of time together. Once the office closes that will be it until after the new year, so that's a solid week of uninterrupted Dom time.

After my bath I lie on our huge bed, snuggled up tight in my huge bathrobe. I feel so warm and comfortable but it's still like being in a hotel, rather than my home. The bath helps me to drift into a deep slumber. Will I ever wake up from this dream?

∞ ∞ ∞

The next morning and I'm still here. I head into the office very early, bright eyed and bushy tailed. It may be the day before Christmas Eve but I'm going to make the most of the day and get some work done. Usually the last few days in the office are filled with gossip, food and any excuse not to do any work, it's Christmas after all, but not today. Today I'm going to work like a boss, because I am the boss.

I may well have fucked up again yesterday but I'm determined to make this work and be better today. Try harder. I go through my emails and make sure everything is as up to date as possible and I'm caught up on the work we're doing for Mark.

At 7.15am Fran comes in, ever the early bird she does a double take, but soon recovers as she walks past my office. I turn my attention back to work and continue on, ignoring the hustle and bustle as the usual nine to fivers appear. In my other life, that was me.

Fran taps sharply on the door.

'Come in,' I singsong, brightly. I've decided not to say anything to Fran, no need to rock the boat. I'll just do better, she was clearly being kind, again. She's saved me twice this week and not said a word about it. She obviously has my back so there's no need to embarrass her.

Fran strides in with Kian in her wake, with everything going on I completely forgot I was supposed to do the rounds and introduce him to everyone in the office. It's customary that the line manager does this in their first week. It also helps fill their time as the first week can be a little monotonous, ensuring they have all the gear and training in place. A lot of reading and watching, but not a lot of doing.

'I've brought Kian, I thought you could show him around?' Fran suggests while Kian looks around the office clearly impressed, shifting from foot to foot awkwardly.

'Ah yes, I'm so sorry about yesterday Kian. I completely lost track of time. Come on, I'll show you around and introduce you to everyone now.' May as well get it over and done with. 'How's your first few days of work been?' I ask, trying to emit an air of professionality so he doesn't think I'm a complete forgetful mess.

'No problem, that would be great.' Kian smiles warmly, I'd forgotten how lovely his Irish accent is. 'My first few days have been good, it's interesting starting at this time of year, so close to Christmas, but I think it'll make it easier when I come back in the new year.'

The office shuts down over the next few weeks with only a skeleton staff keeping everything going. Most people book off two weeks and I'm so excited and ready to have this time. I make idle chitchat with Kian about his previous job and his move from Ireland, he's really rather charming and much to my distain I can see why *he* was offered the job and not me. He has a lot of experience and is clearly very passionate about the role.

I start on our floor and manage to get around, luckily there's no difference where the staff are concerned so there's no uncomfortable incidents of not knowing names. I know the ground floor will be trickier as I generally have less to do with HR and finance.

'Hank is the head of HR; I'll introduce you to him first then he can introduce his team,' I explain to Kian, leading him towards HR's bank of desks. As we get there, I'm finding it hard to locate where Hank sits. I keep looking around for him, he's not usually hard to spot, he's unconventionally tall and his desk is higher than the others so he normally sticks out like a sore thumb. Perhaps he's on holiday already, it is almost Christmas. I notice that a lot of people are on holiday today, and it's not taken me long to introduce Kian around.

'Eve, is Hank around? I ask his second in command, keen to get it over and done with.

'Hank?' she asks, looking puzzled.

'Yes, Hank, the head of HR,' I explain, I'm beginning to feel a bit irritated by this. I've got a lot of work to get back to.

'No, Jeanie is the head of HR,' Eve says, indicating the corner seat where I can see the back of a head I hadn't noticed when we came in. Jeanie, what's Jeanie doing here? It's been almost five years since Jeanie worked here. Did I really make such a difference to Jeanie's life that she decided to stay here? Are we friends? Judging by the Marnie conversation perhaps not. This is going to be awkward.

'Yes, of course,' I say smiling. 'I must've been thinking of someone else.' I wave my hand dismissively but am acutely aware of how crazy I must appear.

Sensing she's being talked about Jeanie turns around. Her hair is in a straight long bob and she's wearing a fitted trouser suit, so very different from her long curly tresses and the boho dresses she usually wears. She looks like a completely different person.

I'm shocked, quite taken aback. It's fine, you can do this, I tell myself. Pretend you don't know her. Pretend you don't know her. I mentally shake myself out of it.

'Hi Jeanie, I'm just introducing Kian, our new manager. This is Jeanie.' I smile politely.

'Hi,' Jeanie says coolly to me. She turns her attention to Kian. 'Lovely to meet you. We've been in touch over email already when arranging your interview. We also do an HR induction so you know the channels in case you need us.' As she says "in case you need us", she casts her eyes in my direction, indicating that it would obviously be my fault if he did.

Jeanie starts to introduce her team members and go over what they each do within the team. I take a sly look at her desk, seeing a picture of Dana and Penny can't help but make my gut ache. It feels weird that I'm not a part of their lives here. Those cheeky little girls, especially Penny and her sassy ways. I think of when she was born so small, I was the first friend to hold her in my arms, it felt so special and I've loved watching her grow and then Dana came along three years later. An absolute doll and the spitting image of her sister but so much calmer. They always make me smile, and I'm missing them so much in this life.

On the other side of her desk is a picture in a really pretty frame, I reposition myself to be able to really scrutinise it and learn about the other Jeanie. Does she have a partner here? Jeanie in real life hasn't dated anyone for years. Swearing off men after a brief holiday romance broke her heart. They'd not known each other long but she was so invested, then he did the dirty on her, it was sad to see her go through that. It would be nice to see her happy here with someone again. Who knows when I go back, perhaps I could help her search him out in my real life, and she'd finally find love? If he actually exists in my real life that is and isn't just a dream man. Not that she needs a man. As she always reminds me, she's perfectly happy as she is, she doesn't need anyone to complete her.

I continue to scrutinise the frame and when the image comes into focus it knocks the air right out of me. I suddenly feel really hot, my mouth goes dry as I go to speak and I close my mouth. I try to stay steady and wait for it to pass, being careful not to draw attention to myself, but it doesn't pass. I start to see dots in front of my eyes and I try desperately to steady myself but it all happens so quickly; my legs begin to feel wobbly and my head swims. I reach out as I begin to fall. Then everything goes black.

Chapter 14

I come to with everyone huddled around me and I'm acutely aware I'm lying on the floor with what feels like someone's coat underneath my head. I stare down and see my skirt is hitched up but no one appears to have taken the decision to cover my modesty, great. I look up, horrified, into Jeanie's staring eyes. What's going on? Where am I?

'Steady there,' says Jeanie as I try to sit up. 'You had quite a fall, are you okay?' She offers me a small smile which is distant from her usual big, toothy grin. I'm pleased to see her and I cling to her hand, I can feel a bit of resistance but she doesn't move it away. Jeanie looks strange and my muddled head struggles to work out what's wrong. Why is my friend being so distant? Where are we?

I look around feeling fuzzyheaded and feel I'm going to be sick, I open my mouth to speak and it bobs open like a goldfish.

'I like your b-b-bob,' I say finally to Jeanie, giving her a big smile.

'Um thanks,' she replies, finally giving me a real smile. That's better. Although I'm confused why Jeanie's in my workplace. 'I think she's a bit disorientated,' Jeanie says quietly and not to me but I'm here and I can hear her.

'We've called an ambulance they should be on their way,' says Kian in his soft Irish accent, attempting to pat me on the shoulder awkwardly.

Everything comes back into focus and I'm mortified. I instantly let go of Jeanie's hand, embarrassed for the intrusion on her personal space. I've remembered where I am now, and in this world Jeanie and I are not best friends.

I've caused a massive scene with my fainting. I try to focus on why I fainted, what was I doing just before? As I look around, I recognise where I am. We're in the HR department at work and Jeanie is still here? Jeanie never went away and travelled? I shake my head trying to steady my thoughts, why wouldn't she have gone travelling? It seems so long ago now that she worked here and we were never here at the same time. We often mused about the fun we would have had if we had worked together, lunching and sending each other messages but that's not the world we live in here and I feel sad it's not what we had imagined.

Another wave of nausea engulfs me and I find myself lurching forward as I try desperately to stop anything from coming up.

'Someone fetch her something to throw up in and a glass of water,' shouts Jeanie. So level-headed in a crisis situation.

'What… what happened?' I finally croak out.

'You were introducing me to Jeanie and you just passed out,' explains Kian, indicating over to Jeanie's desk and that's when I see it.

The framed picture of what is presumably Jeanie's wedding day. I always imagined she'd meet someone eventually who would knock her socks off but I never expected this. She's practically glowing in the image; she looks so beautiful. I'd be so happy for her if it wasn't for one detail – the person in the picture who is smiling serenely and looking deep into her eyes is none other than Jake. My Jake.

Jake and Jeanie. Jeanie and Jake? What the fuck?

I want to ask Jeanie what happened. Why is she married to my husband? But I remind myself he's not my husband here. I can't help but feel the rough pangs of jealousy. Has there been something going on between them all along? I thought I was happier here with Dom, but am I if I feel such rage at this situation?

I get myself up on wobbly, Bambi legs and take a seat that someone has pulled up close by. There's a flurry of movement and confusion as I do this. I can tell they're not sure if I should be moving but don't want to argue with me. This is so humiliating.

It's clear to me Jeanie and I are not friends because Jeanie and Jake are together. I would have never guessed they'd end up together. They're so different. Jeanie so wild and free and Jake so calm and into his routines. Perhaps opposites do attract.

Kian scurries off and moments later Fran turns up looking flustered.

'Are you okay, Lena? Do you want us to call anyone?' I can't help but glance at Jeanie as she says this. Normally it would be Jake and if not Jake then Jeanie or my mum. Who would I call here? No point in calling Dom, he's in London and I don't know the names of the Blonde or Redhead so that's no good but my mum is still my mum, even if my friends are not my friends.

'Could you call my mum?' I ask, feeling like a child.

'Dom's away on business in London,' I offer by way of explanation, but they already know that. Fran hurries over to a desk and picks up the phone.

Another flurry of movement and the paramedics arrive. It's becoming more and more of a circus and I can feel my cheeks begin to burn again. Please don't pass out again. The paramedic checks me over and decides he'd like me to come in the ambulance with him and see a doctor. Just to be on the safe side. My mind is racing, is there something wrong with me? Apart from falling into a strange parallel universe, of course.

I try to close my eyes and pull myself back into my happy place but Jeanie and Jake have changed it. I can't help but go back to my wedding day, well my wedding day with Jake, and instead of calming me I can't seem to catch my breath. As I start to hyperventilate the paramedic puts a mask over my face and tells me to breathe slowly, he counts it out with me but I'm finding it increasingly hard to concentrate. My heart is pounding against my chest, am I having a heart attack? With that thought my breathing becomes faster and I don't know how to make it stop.

'You're okay, I think you're just having a panic attack. You need to breathe slowly, Lena. Come on concentrate, breathe in with me…… and out.'

As the paramedic tries to calm me, I lock eyes with Jeanie. Who is she in this world? She can see the panic in my eyes and moves closer mirroring the paramedics breathing. Finally, my breathing is back down, I'm exhausted and feel like I could fall asleep on the office floor.

'Right, let's go. Are you accompanying her?' he asks Jeanie. She looks around awkwardly and rests her gaze on Fran, hoping for an out.

'I'm so sorry, Lena, Mark's in the office this afternoon.' Fran grits her teeth. 'Or I'd come, Jeanie do you think you could go? Mark's a really important client, isn't he, Lena?' she says and I can't help but think back to my massive fuckup.

I nod along silently, concentrating on my breathing not having the energy to answer but hoping that Jeanie will come with me.

'Okay, I'll come with you until your mum gets there. Have we got hold of her yet?' Jeanie looks around as if Mum could appear at any moment.

'Not yet,' says Fran. 'But Kian will keep trying, won't you?' she commands and he nods emphatically. What must Kian think of me? I've hardly been in the office, fucked up an important meeting with a client, forgotten about him and now fainted when I went to show him around.

I can sense all eyes on me in the office and thank God this is happening down here, on the first floor, with the people I don't see every day.

∞ ∞ ∞

I've been sitting on the hospital bed waiting for hours to be seen. They've done some bloods but no one has come back to discuss it yet. Jeanie is sitting awkwardly next to me in a hard-plastic chair. I don't envy her, I bet her back is aching. As if hearing my thoughts, she rubs her back and adjusts herself in the seat. I look around, but there's not much to look at, the room has the usual hospital smell, a mix of sick, poo and disinfectant. The room is bright white, it must've been recently decorated as there's a faint smell of paint too.

We've been sitting mostly in silence after the initial small talk about what's happening at work. I can't believe Jeanie is the head of HR, incredible. She too was just working in admin before and really didn't take it seriously. It wasn't until she came back from travelling that she found her true calling in marketing and has been climbing the ladder ever since.

There's no sign of Mum yet. She's not answering her phone so she probably has it buried away in the bottom of her bag. They've tried her house but there's no answer.

It's kind of nice to be around Jeanie again, although I sense the feeling isn't mutual. She's pleasant but muted, not herself at all. I miss her animated stories and big smile. What happened to us Jeanie? Is it because you married my husband?

'So, you and Jake have anything nice planned for Christmas?' I ask brightly. God, this is awkward, but I'm going to try my best to work out what happened. I'm looking for clues.

'We're visiting his parents and then we have a long weekend away for New Year's, it's our wedding anniversary,' she says almost flinching, shrugging her shoulders apologetically.

I think of Jake's parents, does his mum like Jeanie? Our relationship is strained at best. Jake is their only child and they completely dote on him, it's absolutely adorable but also means that no one is ever good enough for him. Perhaps that includes Jeanie? Or is it just me? My house is never clean enough and the fact they don't have grandchildren yet is a constant bone of contention.

'Oh yes, how long's it been?' I ask, innocently.

'Six years,' she says, closing the conversation and

looking down at a particularly interesting scuff on the floor.

I'm slightly clearer on when they got together, that would put their wedding over a year after our non-wedding. I sit pondering what to ask her. This woman who was my best friend but is now married to my husband. Did I find out they were cheating? Did she always hold a torch for him? I have no idea. Yes, they were friends but I never saw them as anything more. How could this have happened? The rage has started to bubble up in my chest and I can't help but blurt it out.

'So were you two together behind my back,' I spit angrily. This may all be old news to Jeanie but it feels like the huge betrayal has just happened for me. And it stings like a dagger in my heart. How could she?

Jeanie looks up, shocked by my sudden outburst and apparent change of personality. 'What the fuck, Lena?' she starts, narrowing her eyes with steely determination. Have we had this conversation before?

'Answer the question,' I say bluntly, tired of the pleasantries. What's the point in pretending anymore?

'You know we weren't together behind your fucking back. You chose that arsehole Dom. Jake was devastated.' The venom in her voice is not something I've heard before.

'Oh, but you were there, weren't you? You were supposed to be my friend,' I spit, the hurt biting into me. I never expected this of her. How could she be with him?

Jeanie stands, beginning to gather her things, apparently silenced by my outburst. I'm enraged, why won't she answer me.

'Bitch,' I mutter under my breath.

Jeanie stops and looks at me, clearly, I didn't say it

quietly enough. She turns on her heels and shouts, 'Don't you dare play the victim.' She visibly calms herself and continues, lowering her voice. 'You never were the victim in any of this. You were supposed to be *my* friend but you left me and Marnie to tell everyone you weren't coming to the wedding. Marnie told your mum and dad; do you know that? They were crushed, it was awful.'

I wince at the thought of disappointing them, especially Dad, he's not here anymore for me to make it right. Were we okay before he died? I suddenly want to cry but I stop myself, not now.

Jeanie isn't done yet. 'I had the wonderful job of telling Jake and I will never forgive you for that. The worst bit is that you never said anything to me or Marnie, you just disappeared.'

I look down at my hands in my lap after this revelation. I'm ashamed. Would I have done that? Not even told him I wasn't coming? But it wasn't me, I remind myself, it was this Lena, this different Lena.

Jeanie is on a roll now, still going on; it seems as though this has been something she has held onto for a long time. 'You swanned off with Dom without a thought for anyone else and I didn't hear from you for weeks, not that I wanted to. Then you came back thinking everything would be fine and it wasn't a big deal, no. Jake shut himself away for months, he was heartbroken. It took a long time to piece him back together and yes I helped, and yes we fell in love,' she spits. 'Not that it's any of *your* business,' Jeanie shouts, no longer able to control her temper. She stomps out and as she tries to swish the curtain closed behind her she's greeted by a doctor trying to come into the cubicle.

'Sorry,' she says, her harsh tones changing, it almost comes out as a whisper. She shuffles past the doctor at speed, her head down.

The doctor tries to pretend she didn't hear any of it, but it's evident she did just like the entire A&E must have heard.

'Do you have anyone else coming for you?' the doctor asks.

'Not yet, still trying to get hold of my mum,' I explain. 'Is there something wrong?' Oh my God, in all of this I hadn't even thought of that. Why does someone need to be here? Is she about to tell me I'm dying? Or I've had some kind of stroke? Maybe that's why I'm in this weird dream world. Am I in a coma? I begin to feel the walls close in and I try to take deep, steadying breaths.

'Nothing to worry about,' the doctor says, raising her hand and sensing my rising panic. 'We've run some tests; we think it's because of the pregnancy. Have you been overdoing it recently?' she asks. 'Your blood pressure is a little low and you're anaemic but we can help with that. Have you been taking your antenatal vitamins?'

I blink rapidly, trying to take in what the doctor has just said. Pregnancy?

'I..I..I'm pregnant?' I stammer, placing my hand over my mouth.

'Yes, didn't you know?' She smiles reassuringly.

A surge of nausea engulfs me as if to confirm it and I think I'm going to throw up. I wretch and the doctor grabs a cardboard dish from a trolley behind me, but nothing comes up. I don't know if it's the pregnancy or the shock. How did I not see the signs?

'Do you want me to call anyone for you?' she asks,

looking more concerned. 'Is this welcome news?'

'No, no this is great news. I'm thrilled. Just surprised, that's all.'

Just then my mum comes breezing in.

'Oh darling, are you okay? What's happened? I heard you fainted in front of everyone at work.' She gestures wildly, ever theatrical. 'You poor love, you know that happened to me once. It was the worst.' Everything's about Mum again. I almost smile.

'Not everyone, Mum,' I say, playing it down. 'Just the first floor.' I ignore her attempt to tell one of her stories.

'So, doctor, what is it? Why did my daughter faint?' she asks, not one to care too deeply about privacy.

'I'll leave it to Lena to fill you in,' says the doctor, smiling at me. 'I'll be back shortly with a prescription for some iron tablets. We're also going to send you over for a scan, just to check up on everything.'

'Oh, are you anaemic. Is that why you fainted? It's all that not eating meat rubbish,' Mum says rolling her eyes, clearly my decision to be vegetarian here didn't go down well with her. 'What's the scan for?'

'Yes, I'm anaemic, but it's not necessarily because I'm a vegetarian. I'm pregnant, hence the scan.' I wait for her big reaction because this has been a long time coming and Mum's reaction doesn't disappoint. She flings her arms around me, never mind the empty sick bowl. As she pulls away, I can see tears running down her face which she dabs at.

'Oh, this is fantastic news.' She looks down at my stomach. 'Must be very early days, what a few weeks?'

'I don't know,' I admit, not quite believing it myself. It must be very early though. Mum takes my hand and gives it a big squeeze. I'm so happy she's here, she may be dramatic but she's warm and kind and I'm glad to have someone who loves me with me.

∞ ∞ ∞

Down in the early pregnancy unit I'm feeling nervous about the scan.

'So, looking at the measurements, I'd put you at about thirteen weeks. You really had no idea? No symptoms?' the sonographer asks. 'Your stomach is small but you may be carrying further back. You'd be surprised sometimes people just pop overnight. Everything looks healthy though. I assume you've not been taking your antenatal vitamins or had any appointments with the midwives?'

I shake my head, overwhelmed with the news. I'm going to have a baby with Dom.

Mum is flabbergasted at how far along I am and is momentarily silenced. She soon recovers. 'This happened to her up the street you know.'

'What happened to her up the street?' I ask, already sensing I don't want to know the answer.

'Didn't know she was pregnant, went to the toilet one day, had the baby. Great fat thing she was though, not like you. No wonder she didn't know she was pregnant.'

I roll my eyes, not wanting to get into idle gossip about the goings on in my mum's street. She's obsessed, her curtain is forever twitching, she knows everything about everyone. I think it became worse after Dad died, a way of escapism, her own personal soap opera. Mum's big personality and warm ways mean that people often confide in her and she loves it.

'Although, I'm surprised at you. After all you have

been pregnant before. You should have seen the signs.'

Chapter 15

Mum's words are echoing in my ears as I think back to the first time. It was unexpected. It wasn't planned and wished for, but I knew straight away that something was wrong. I felt sick and bloated and finally I realised I'd missed a period. I took the test on my own, reassuring myself I wasn't pregnant. It couldn't be that. I was taking the test to rule it out, so it was okay that I hadn't told anyone. No one really needed to know. How silly would I look when it was negative?

My shock as both lines appeared was intense. The first dark line was strong but the second was faint. What did that mean? Was I pregnant? I googled and searched and my fears were confirmed. If the pregnancy hormone wasn't there, there'd be no line, so I was pregnant. Probably very early. Still not ready to face facts I bought another test this time with words instead of lines. There would be no ambiguity then. I took the test and the words showed on the screen PREGNANT.

I was shocked with a mixture of happy and sad. I cried myself to sleep with the idea of having to tell him. What would he say? Was I ready for my life to change so completely? Did I even know what I was getting myself into? We hadn't been together that long, is this what he would want?

Jake took it amazingly well. He was kind and supportive and it's part of what made me fall more in love with him. He didn't pressure me to keep it or to get rid of it, but I knew he wanted to have the baby and I loved that he wanted that. As I hesitated over my future the decision was ripped from my hands, no sooner had I taken the test and realised than fate had a different idea. I began to miscarry; I was with Mum at the time that's why she knew. I came out of the bathroom crying and she wrapped her arms around me quietly, so out of character for her, and let me sob until no tears were left.

Jake came next and he was so kind. We cried together over everything that had been taken from us. The disappointment, but in amongst it there was relief and I couldn't help but feel guilty about that. A few months later he proposed, the man I'd imagined a baby with and now we had another chance. Perhaps we could have that baby later down the line, we weren't ready yet we agreed but we loved each other and we wanted to get married, it was the right decision. I said yes.

∞ ∞ ∞

The second time was worse. We had been married for over three years when we decided to try again, having focused on our careers, home, travel and just being us. It took over a year to conceive, we'd done it before when we weren't even trying, we told ourselves, so we could do it again. Why was it taking so long? Eventually it happened, after many months of hope my period was late, I was at last pregnant.

But this time was even shorter, I miscarried at five weeks. I probably wouldn't have even noticed or so said the doctors, just thought it was a heavy period if I hadn't been monitoring it so closely and taken a test. That was of no comfort to me. It felt cruel, this time was planned, this time we'd done everything right and still no baby. My heart ached for me and for Jake.

I wanted to try again immediately but Jake said no. He said his heart couldn't take it right away, he needed time. I knew all about time, I could feel it ticking away. Tick. Tock. Tick. Tock. Would I miss my chance? We were already four years into our marriage. People had already begun to ask questions. Everyone had started to have babies. Were we planning on having kids? Better get to it. When? How many did we want? The pain of those questions never went away. Assuming we hadn't decided to try yet, asking the question as though it hadn't already occurred to us.

It took over a year and a half before we started again and another six months to conceive. This was surely the one. If it wasn't, we were going to have to go for tests. We'd become pregnant before so, so far, they were reluctant to do tests, and it was common to miscarry, they said.

As if that would ease my pain, they wouldn't see me before the third time. We were there though. Over six years into our marriage and I was pregnant and it was at the twelve-week mark. We'd begun to tell people; we were excited but then I had a scan and they couldn't find the heartbeat. I began to bleed heavily. It was over. We were both sad, but Jake recovered quickly. Did he not care anymore? He didn't want to go back to the doctors yet but he said soon. When was that? What about what I wanted? And so here we are. He can't even remember our anniversary anymore, he's with Jeanie here and now I'm pregnant with Dom's baby. Is this a sign that we were never meant to be?

Is that why I couldn't carry our babies?

Chapter 16

'Are you sure you don't fancy coming to mine for some lunch or we could go out?' Mum asks, her eyes showing her concern. We're in the car after being discharged, I've been told to take it easy and make some doctor's appointments as soon as possible.

'No thank you, Mum. I just want to go home and have a good rest. I'm knackered.' I am knackered but I'm also freaking out, a mixture of elation and sadness has engulfed me and I can barely find the words to convey to my mum how I'm feeling.

I don't know what happened here, whether Dom and I were trying for a long time or whether we'd almost given up too but I do know the two of us can make a baby together and that's got to mean something, right? And we've obviously been here before, or Mum would never have mentioned it.

Were Jake and I so totally incompatible? None of our babies survived. I need time to process all this and I need to do it alone, without my Mum's theatrics.

'Okay, sweetheart. A baby, imagine me a Grandma. How exciting.' Her eyes glow at the secret, she's the first to know and she's revelling in it. 'Oh, just wait until I tell Stella.' She gives me a knowing look and I can't help but roll my eyes. Stella and Mum have a real love, hate relationship. Best friends since they moved in next door. Mum's going to love that she knew first.

'Sorry, Mum, but you can't tell Stella,' I plead.

'Why not? She's my friend,' she says indignantly, if her hands weren't on the steering wheel they'd be on her hips.

'She's also Dom's mother so that trumps friend and we'll be the ones to tell her when the time's right,' I say sternly, knowing it will be hard for Mum to keep this secret. She can enjoy telling the whole street when the time is right.

'But you're already thirteen weeks, it's not like before. She can know now, it doesn't matter,' Mum says, her eyes flicking between me and the road.

'I think it matters if Dom doesn't know yet, don't you? *We'll* tell her and that's final. And we'll tell her when we decide to.'

Mum probably already has ideas about the reveal, but I don't want anything fancy. Just telling them with Dom would be perfect. I can't help but smile at the thought of telling people. I'm further along than I've ever been and we heard the heartbeat. I still can't help but feel worried about keeping this one safe, making sure they're okay. I need to look after myself and make sure I do everything right this time. Everyone said it wasn't my fault, but maybe if I had done something differently, I wouldn't have miscarried.

'You could announce it on Christmas Day, at ours,' Mum says, cutting into my thoughts. Her eyes light up at the thought of the drama of it all. So, we're spending Christmas at Mum's all together, how lovely. I may not have Marnie and Jeanie but I could get on board with a big family Christmas. Especially with a mother-in-law who loves me, which Jake's mum never has.

'I could make a banner. Or you could give me the scan photo and I could get a bigger photo done of it for us to present to her,' Mum continues, the excitement evident in her voice.

I begin to imagine telling people. It's exciting to think about it, I only told Jeanie and Marnie before. No one at work knew, they didn't know when it went away either. I could pretend like it never happened, but now it's different. I'm past the crucial point and although I'm not showing yet I'm sure it'll only be a matter of time. I'll need to tell work so I can go to all my appointments. I look down at my stomach and I can feel something swimming around in there, is it my imagination or is that the baby?

'That's lovely, Mum, thank you. I think we'll probably do something more low-key but I'll give you one to keep for you. I need the rest for Dom. Please don't tell anyone about the baby until I'm ready,' I reiterate, smiling serenely at her, hoping she won't get offended and make it about her.

'Okay, I won't.' She smiles at me but I can tell she thinks I'm ruining her fun.

As we pull up to the house, I give Mum a quick hug and jump out of the car, looking forward to being alone with my thoughts.

'Thank you for everything today, I'll call you later,' I say, closing the car door and practically sprinting to my front door. I just want to snuggle into bed and think everything through. I don't want there to be any hint of Mum coming in because she will pounce on it and stay all afternoon.

∞ ∞ ∞

Once inside, I go to the kitchen and fling open the cupboards to find some bread to make toast. I scoff it down without a second thought for my looks. This amazing body I've cultivated will be being put through its paces in a completely different way soon and I need to fuel it up properly. No more vegetarianism for me, I'm going back to meat. I hope Dom won't make it into an issue, he seems so supportive that I'm sure he won't care. I'm thinking of the baby and the nutrients it needs, after all.

I think about telling Dom, I bet he'll be so excited. I wonder if he'll cry. I think back to Jake finding out about the second pregnancy, he cried with happy tears, so excited for our miracle baby at last but it was not to be.

I don't know if Dom and I have struggled to conceive too, so I'll have to handle it sensitively. I'll definitely wait until he's back in person. Thinking of Dom, I pull out my phone and gaze at his handsome face. I tap out a quick message to him telling him I can't wait to see him when he gets home and I'm looking forward to spending Christmas together. I feel as though everything is falling into place but it's not the place I'd expected. After my toast I take myself up to bed and fall into a deep sleep, dreaming of what mine and Dom's baby might look like.

Chapter 17

I'm woken by a loud banging and I cover my head with my pillow but I know who it is. I scold myself, why didn't I think to message him last night? I roll over but this guy is not giving up. I sigh, pulling the sheets back and jump out of bed. There will be no work out for me today, that I'm sure of, but I now need to go and convince Brad. I hope I don't have to tell him about the baby, it seems wrong to tell him before Dom.

I have a quick look in the mirror and grab my dressing gown. Instead of smoothing my hair down I rough it up a bit more before running my fingers along the puffy bags under my eyes; perhaps this won't be so difficult after all. I heave open the door and Brad is there looking unimpressed, furiously thumbing through his phone, presumably he was about to start calling me.

'Having a lie in, were we?' he mutters, shrugging his huge shoulders and placing his shovel like hands on his hips. He walks over to the grass not looking at me. 'This is a double session, luckily, but we are running behind now.' He returns to his professional tone, looking up, ready for business. I scuttle behind him aware of how ridiculous I look in my dressing gown in the front garden. Does he really expect me to do my workout dressed like this?

'I'm not feeling well. I'm sorry Brad. Obviously we'll still pay but I need to cancel today.' A huge sigh of relief escapes as I finish the sentence. Surely that's the end of it.

This riles Brad and he pulls himself up to his full height. He's rather imposing and I suddenly feel the urge to run back inside.

'I don't know what's up with you recently,' he says through gritted teeth. Brad starts to lecture me about the importance of looking after myself and not overdoing it on the wines. Hilariously, I won't be drinking anything from now on, but he doesn't know that.

'I know, I'm really sorry. I'll try to do better,' I say trying to end the conversation, I suddenly feel really nauseous and I'm keen to get back inside. I feel bad, it's not Brad's fault and he's come here for my usual workout to find out it was a wasted journey, I'd be mad too.

'I just don't know if I can do this anymore,' he says putting his huge hands through his hair and rubbing his face.

It seems crazy to drop me as a client just for missing or forgetting about a few sessions. I go to speak but Brad isn't finished and I stand there holding it in whilst he waffles on about healthy living, it's hard to concentrate on what he's saying because I feel so sick. It's as if now I know the baby's there all of the symptoms have come on threefold.

'Well?' Brad asks bringing me back from my thoughts. I go to answer him but a wave of nausea engulfs me again and as I try to turn back towards the house Brad steps forward blocking my path, it's no use, it's coming up, I projectile vomit all over Brad. It puddles on his trainers and I can see lumps splashed up his bare legs. I bet he wishes he had trousers on today. I put my hand over my mouth, unsure what to do.

Brad's face is a picture. He keeps looking down at what were his crisp white running shoes and then back at me. As he does, I see his hand come up to his mouth. The smell is really, really bad, then suddenly and violently Brad starts to throw up too. This big man can't take a bit of sick. I almost want to laugh.

'Oh, Brad, I'm so sorry.' I put my hands out towards him then step back and retract them, I don't want to be covered in *his* sick. I stifle a laugh, it's almost comical and I can see by Brad's change in stance this angers him further.

Brad doesn't even look at me but puts his huge paw up in front of his face, covering his mouth and slowly starts to walk away. Well, I guess that's the end of that. No double session for me now. I look down at the sick and decide to deal with that later, I hope it rains so I don't have to. I wrap the dressing gown around me to keep out the chill and head back indoors.

Instead of a PT session, we had a throwing up session in the front garden, I bet it looked hilarious if you were watching. I think of Mum and her curtain twitching and hope none of my neighbours were able to see our weird vomit-off.

Poor Brad. I'm mortified. I tap out a quick message apologising again and saying I'll pay him twice over for the double session, so he can get his trainers professionally cleaned. The poor guy, who'd have thought someone so huge would have such a sensitive stomach.

Now I've thrown up I feel much better and a bit

peckish really. I head into the kitchen, gleeful at the prospect of eating whatever I like. It really doesn't matter anyway, because I have to stop PT now I'm pregnant. Or perhaps we could do pregnancy friendly sessions. If only our session had been after I'd told Dom we could have discussed it.

∞ ∞ ∞

Today's the day, Christmas Eve, Dom will be home soon and I can tell him about the baby. I'm giddy with excitement. A perfect start to Christmas. I can feel fluttering again and I put my hand on my stomach savouring the feeling. I don't know if it's nerves, excitement or the actual baby but I keep feeling waves of nausea.

I shoot off a quick message to Dom asking when he'll be back and get myself ready to go into work. Because it's Christmas Eve I know I won't need to do much, and we'll be finishing early. No one expects a lot, I just need to hold in my little secret until Dom gets back this afternoon, not long to wait now. Maybe we'll tell people at the party tonight, although we'll probably want to wait and tell the rest of our family first. I hope he doesn't mind Mum knowing first. But how can he object? He wasn't here and I didn't know.

∞ ∞ ∞

The morning goes by quickly, filled with a tiny amount of work and a lot of chatting about what everyone's up to over Christmas and what they're looking forward to in the New Year. It's all very jolly and I can't help but think of next Christmas when the baby will be here. I

126

try to imagine Dom as a Dad but at the same time my mind wanders back to all the times I've imagined Jake as a Dad. He would be a great Dad too.

Dom messages in the afternoon to say the trains are delayed and he expects he'll have to meet me at the Christmas party, so to get ready and go on without him and he'll see me there.

I spend ages picking through my clothes for the perfect outfit, trying on everything and imagining myself with a bump. Fortunately, I don't have to worry about showing yet. I put my hand on my stomach, where are you hiding little baby?

∞ ∞ ∞

I arrive at the party dressed in a deep red dress and feeling full of Christmas cheer. I'd been dreading the party, listening to everyone's joy whilst Jake and I still battled on, but now, with Dom, it feels completely different. I have to mentally force myself not to touch my stomach, even though all I want to do is pat it, knowing that there's a little baby in there. I dodge the wines, instead discreetly helping myself to an apple juice, disguising it in a wine glass so I don't have to answer questions about not drinking all night.

'You look lovely.' Eli smiles, no backhanded compliment in sight but it feels insincere. At least I knew where I stood with Eli before, but this version of him is sickly sweet and I find it hard to believe anything he says.

'Thank you, and you too,' I answer, smiling sweetly.

'Where's Dom? Is he not with you?' he asks, I turn my head to the door at the mention of his name.

'No, should be here any minute now though. His

train was delayed,' I explain, feeling giddy at the thought of Dom's arrival.

'Oh, really?' He looks puzzled. 'I thought I saw him at work when I was leaving about three.' He rolls his eyes; Eli would hate having to stay that late on Christmas Eve. Everyone always leaves around noon. If I'd been working with him, I'd never have heard the end of it. If it's true, it's his own fault, he's thorough but slow and he pays almost too much attention to detail.

'Oh, well he's probably popped home to get ready.' I grasp at straws but something about it makes me feel uneasy. Even though Eli is trying to pretend to be kind, I can see he's loving this. The drama, the intrigue. Undoubtedly, he has stored this away in his gossip bank. He carefully keeps the smirk from his face and purses his lips, presumably trying to keep his usual biting comments at bay.

'Yes, I'm sure,' he says, appeasing me. But I'm not appeased, why was he here at 3pm? When he's not even told me he's home yet. Last I heard he was on the train and delayed. I start to feel queasy and I cringe at the memory of Brad covered in mine and then his own vomit. The horror on his face was a picture. I don't want a repeat of that.

'I'm just going to the ladies.' I excuse myself and rush to the cloakroom. I can feel the bile rising in my stomach and I just make it into the cubicle in time as I retch away.

I come out wiping my hands to find Fran at the sinks. I try to remember if she was in here when I hurried in but I'm not sure.

'Not feeling well?' Fran asks kindly.

'You could say that,' I say, giving her a knowing

smile. At my answer she abruptly turns her whole body towards me and appraises me, clearly looking at my stomach. It only takes a woman of appropriate age, speaking of feeling sick in the office for everyone to assume she's pregnant, so her hearing me throw up will surely give her a clue. I almost don't care if Fran knows now, fuck it, Dom couldn't be bothered to tell me he's home. I don't see what would be so pressing in the office on Christmas Eve that he had to go there before coming home and I've not even seen him yet.

'You don't mean…' she says in hushed tones, her eyes looking around the cloakroom conspiratorially.

'Yes, I do,' I say, patting my stomach and grinning from ear to ear. It feels so good to tell someone and although normally Fran would be one of the last people I'd want to tell, here she really does feel like a friend. Just goes to show, people can surprise you.

'Wow, I didn't realise you were…' She stops herself and smiles. 'Well congratulations, how exciting. When are you due?'

'They think late June, early July time.' Telling Fran, I can't help but imagine telling Jeanie and Marnie and how excited they'd be for me. But here I won't and it feels sad.

'Wow, it's just so unexpected,' Fran muses and I wonder if I had troubles here too and had already confided in Fran. 'I always thought you and Dom would just, jet set around, no kids,' she explains. 'Terribly happy of course, who needs kids,' she half backtracks but then realises what she's said.

'Well that's the thing, I didn't realise,' I confide. 'But I'm sure Dom will be thrilled. He'll make a great Dad.'

Fran turns to dry her hands, turning on the loud hand dryers and ending our conversation. She turns on her heels but just before she leaves, she smiles at me.

'*Will* be thrilled? So, Dom doesn't actually know yet?' she asks, furrowing her brow.

'Not yet.' I smile at the thought of telling him.

And with that she wanders through the door and back into the party. I almost wish she'd stayed so we could talk about it more but I know we can't realistically stay in the ladies all night.

I finish cleaning myself up and swirl some water around in my mouth. I'm not sure about the pregnancy glow, I look rather peaky and flushed. Is it glowing hot, because I'm getting that or perhaps that was my chat with Fran? I think to how Marnie and Jeanie would have reacted, arms thrown around me, probably a lunch, I don't think I'll get that here but it was still nice.

∞ ∞ ∞

Back in the party my mind is on Dom, I scour the room for him. I know he's back, so why hasn't he come to find me? As I'm searching, I walk slowly around, the room has been *Christmas'd* up, tinsel and holly everywhere and there's an array of Christmas jumpers. I smile at the people I know but don't linger for too long. I don't want to get pulled into a conversation.

I decide to check my phone, perhaps he's messaged me. I pull it out my handbag still mid-walk and someone knocks it right out of my hand, it drops to the floor and I almost fall over in the process. I bend down to retrieve it and butt heads with the idiot who should watch where he's going. As I'm about to say that to the imbecile, I look up into big brown eyes. Eyes that I've known and looked into for the longest time.

'Jake,' I rasp.

Chapter 18

He looks good, his hair is longer than normal, but his usual splattering of stubble is still there. He's dressed smartly, clearly making an effort for Jeanie and I swallow back the lump in my throat caused by just looking at him. My heart is hammering in my chest as I think about all our time together, and the pain we went through, but it's not the same for him.

As he steps back, rubbing his head Jeanie moves forward from behind him holding his hand. They look at each other and smile. A secret smile between lovers, not friends. I know I'm not entitled, but it breaks my heart a little bit. I unconsciously feel my hand heading towards my stomach, ready to stroke the non-existent bump in the knowledge that a much-wanted baby is inside, but I fight the urge.

'Hello, Lena,' Jake drawls, his voice deep as he offers a small tight smile.

Even though I know him so well, he feels like a total stranger. His gestures and mannerisms towards me have changed, he feels closed off. Separate from me. Although we've felt apart for so long, now for a change, I don't know what's going on in his mind. I don't know how he feels about me, it's intriguing and troubling. I find myself constantly looking between Jeanie and Jake, they're holding hands and he's come to the Christmas Eve party. He hates the Christmas Eve party. He never came for me. But did I ever really want him to?

'How are you feeling now?' Jeanie cuts in through gritted teeth, trying her hardest to be kind. I wonder if the two of them have spoken about me at home. In *their* home. It hurts to see they're happy without me. Happy together. Are they better off without me?

'Yes, better, thank you,' I say, lowering my head at the memory of our argument yesterday. Does he still care about me? Does she? Do they miss me? Did she tell him what I said?

The conversation comes to a halt as we all awkwardly sip from our drinks. What now? Do we stay and chat? Or continue on our very separate paths.

As we lower our glasses our fate is decided as Jeanie's phone starts to ring. She excuses herself and heads over to the corner of the room so she can hear better over the humdrum of chattering. I'm left with Jake. Alone.

The atmosphere closes in and I stare at this man. He seems so different, his clothes, even his smell has changed; Jeanie's influence, not mine. It's funny how being with another person can bring out something different in you. There's something about him that looks completely different, but I can't quite put my finger on it. I'm struggling with my feelings for him. I thought I was happier with Dom but seeing Jake in person has thrown me. Our love was not especially romantic but familiar and friendly. Well, until recently. The jealousy I feel is unexpected and it stings, does this mean I'd rather be with Jake.

'How's Dom?' Jake asks flatly, looking past me as if

the mention of his name might summon him.

'He's great,' I say brightly. But I don't know how he is or where he is for that matter, but I won't let Jake know there may be problems. I obviously made my choice here. I look at Jake, so seemingly happy. Here for his wife. I'd told him I wasn't coming this year. I wasn't feeling in the Christmassy mood myself. I wanted to hide away and not do anything. Although my spirit has certainly changed since all of this has happened.

As we both fumble for something to say, or an excuse to leave, Jeanie comes back over.

'The babysitter's had some kind of emergency.' Jeanie crosses her arms. 'Teenagers,' she shrugs. 'Probably been dumped by her boyfriend. We need to head back. I tried to call your mum but she's not picking up. Bye, Lena.'

And they're gone.

Babysitter? Jeanie calling Jake's mum? Jake and Jeanie are parents? My head begins to spin and I make my way over to the tables and take a seat, trying to slow my breathing and think of my happy place, but my happy place is so confused it only makes things worse. Remember the baby, remember the baby. It's okay, it's okay.

As I try to gulp down the bile rising in my throat again, I finally see Dom. Despite my annoyance at him my heart leaps. It's good to see him. Perhaps he had some important business to attend to and that's why he didn't want me to know he was back yet. He probably wanted to get everything out of the way so we could enjoy Christmas together. I watch him as he searches the room for me, but he doesn't see me sitting in the corner. As I go to get up so we can finally be reunited I watch him settle his gaze on who he has been looking for, and it's not me. It's Fran.

He heads over to Fran and I can see a lot of wild hand gestures from Fran as Dom practically strong arms her around the corner and out of sight. I head over towards them to see what's going on.

As I round the corner, I can hear hushed tones but I catch the end of their conversation, Dom's voice.

'Well, I don't know who the fuck the father is. But it isn't me.'

Chapter 19

'What the hell are you talking about, of course it's yours,' I almost scream as I interrupt their secret meeting. Fran has a face like thunder, what's this got to do with her anyway. I turn to face her head on. 'Why are *you* telling him I'm pregnant? It's my news to give. Not yours.' How could she, I thought she was my friend. I look between the two of them, am I missing something?

'Are you really *that* dense?' she sneers. It's like a switch has flicked and I'm faced with the old Fran. 'Give over, you told me about the baby on purpose. You've known for ages about Dom and I and you thought getting yourself pregnant would put a stop to it,' she spits. 'You make me sick.'

I stand stock still, looking slowly between the pair of them as it all dawns on me. I'd never have even considered them a match, maybe in the real world but not here. Not where Fran is this dowdy version of herself, not when Dom is with me. What's happening in this upside-down world. I look to Dom for a denial, to tell me she's crazy but he just stands there looking sheepish and a bit pissed off.

'This is irrelevant,' he says, gesturing at Fran as if

she's a piece of shit on his shoe. 'Especially seeing as you are *clearly* getting up to no good too. I don't see how you can be pissed off with me for looking elsewhere. The father is probably that dumb trainer of yours. Well good luck, he's not going to be able to provide much is he?' Dom smirks at me. Is he enjoying this?

'No, I'm not. I don't know why you would say that?' I say, tears springing to my eyes. 'I thought everything was good between us.' Didn't I?

'We haven't done it in months, you're clearly only a few weeks. It's not possible.' He raises his hand to dismiss me, stopping me from speaking and storms off leaving Fran and me in his wake.

I'm gobsmacked, I don't know what to say or think. If it's months the baby is his. Or could it be true? Was I having an affair too? Before I can utter another word, he pushes past our co-workers and leaves.

My head begins to hurt at the thought of it all. My tears sting my eyes as I feel the world falling apart around me. I turn back and lock eyes with Fran who also has a stream running down her cheeks. She looks at me and wipes the tears away harshly with the back of her hand. Even more bizarre than seeing the kind side of Fran is seeing the vulnerable side and I know she's hating me seeing this.

We clearly aren't friends despite her play acting.

'You fucking bitch,' Fran growls angrily, back to her usual self. She starts to charge towards me. I back up around the corner trying to shield myself and the baby growing inside me. I fall into Kian, who's huddled at the edge of the make-shift dance floor. The Christmas party is in full swing and as a newcomer he probably feels a bit out of place. He smiles warmly when he sees me but his expression drops when he sees Fran looming behind me, steam practically coming out of her ears.

'Everything okay?' he asks looking between us, trying to work out what's happening.

'She's fine,' Fran snarls. 'She's always fine, because muggins here is doing *everything* for her. While she sits uselessly in the corner office forwarding all the emails to me and going out to lunch with the Barbie dolls.' Fran's face has turned puce with rage. Obviously, her relationship with Dom meant more to her than to him.

'I don't forward all my emails to you,' I say quietly, but I'm not really sure what I do or how I got this far. Is it possible that Fran does all my work? I think to the disaster of a meeting with the clients and her redoing all my work and it all starts to fall into place. I can feel my face colouring with the realisation.

I'm useless at my job.

'Not forwarding them for one week and doing one piece of work, *badly*, doesn't change the pattern. You shouldn't be in that position because you DON'T KNOW WHAT YOU'RE FUCKING DOING,' Fran shouts. Her sudden outburst has quietened the party hubbub and someone has turned the music down to ensure they get a front row seat to the show. I almost expect someone to start filming so they can stick it on YouTube. Maybe they are.

Fran turns and stares everyone down. 'WHAT?' she shouts. 'Don't look shocked, you all know I do everything around here. She's only in that position because Dom promoted her into it not because she deserves it.' She points at me with such force it looks like she could damage her arm. Fran looks somewhat pleased at my stunned expression. I thought I'd worked my way to the top but apparently, I slept my way there. 'Don't give me that look. Did you know I get paid more than you? You might well be the "boss"' she scowls, using her fingers to do arm quotes around boss. 'But I'm the real boss, I'm who everyone comes to. I'm the one who does the work. This company would fall apart without me and you know it. And you know what? I can't wait to watch it happen. I quit. You can tell your arsehole husband that too. Good luck with the baby, who's ever it is. Poor bastard.' Fran marches past me, almost knocking me over in her wake. She holds her head high, mollified that she's had the last word and struts out of the party.

Everyone is watching me, waiting for my reaction. Now everyone knows I'm pregnant and it's not the joyous moment I had envisioned. Kian looks at me flabbergasted; what must he think of this company that he's just come into?

Cat fights on Christmas Eve.

Eli comes rushing over, first on the scene, sure he'll get all the gossip, but my mouth's closed. I don't have anything to say. The music is turned back up and people begin to return to their conversations, although I'm sure all of those conversations are centred around Fran and me.

'Are you okay?' Eli says, his voice full of over the top concern, he's loving this.

'I'm okay,' I say quietly, keeping my head down. 'I think I'm going to just head home.'

Eli nods solemnly. 'Okay, I'll wait with you. You can go back to the party Kian,' he says, gesturing with his hand.

'Oh, okay. Are you sure? I don't mind dropping you back if you like.' Kian asks kindly.

'No, no you stay,' I say. 'I don't want to ruin anyone else's evening.'

Eli leads me to the door quietly, people step aside, giving me a wide berth as I come through, it's like the parting of the red seas. I know Eli just wants the gossip but I can't help but feel glad he's trying to be there for me.

Outside in the fresh air it all starts to sink in. This is a fucking messed up world. I look down at my stomach, the only good thing that's keeping me going.

I don't know who's you are but I'm glad you're here.

Chapter 20

I head home wondering whether I should be gearing up for round two. I really don't have the energy to fight with Dom. My blood boils at the thought of him telling Fran the baby isn't his. Of course, it's his, who else's would it be? I've never cheated on Jake and I can't imagine me cheating on Dom. Then I think back to the day this all began, when I was in Dom's office, the kiss and the possibility something more could have happened. But I didn't allow it. I'm not like that. I'm not unfaithful.

Am I?

A niggling doubt makes me wonder, could it be someone else's? I dismiss it, he was thrown because I found out about his little affair and lashed out at me, the arsehole. He'd say anything.

As I arrive home, I can't see any lights on and Dom's car isn't on the drive. Has he gone back to Fran or perhaps he has other fancy ladies? It appears all that glitters isn't gold? It's Christmas Eve and this feels like one of the worst ever, perhaps trumped only by last Christmas. I think back to Jake and imagine him tucking in his and Jeanie's children, it seems he has everything and I have nothing in this cruel world.

I wander into the house, switching on the lights, what was once stylish and modern now looks cold and stark. I long for the comfort of my house with Jake, the clutter, the mess, the knickknacks and pictures on the wall and most of all Spence. I really miss that little pest. I see Ginger sneak by and she momentarily stops and hisses at me. I get it cat; I'm not welcome here. I don't think very much of you either.

I can hardly believe Fran, clearly a leopard doesn't change its spots but simply dresses them in ugly clothing. She's really no different to usual, looking out for herself alone. Having an affair with Dom. I never thought of them in that way and I can't get my head around it here. Dom has always gone for such glamourous women; Fran would be one of them in our world but here it seems odd. I don't know why I was blind to his selfish ways.

All those women he paraded in the office; whose benefit were they for? Who else brings dates into the office, it's just weird? My Dom bubble has officially been burst. We're not meant to be. I think back to how smug I'd felt; look at me, Dom can change for me but he can't change for anyone because he doesn't want to. How deluded I was.

I wander through the house, I'm not really sure what I'm looking for but even though I'm exhausted my legs feel restless. Dom has clearly been here, leaving a mess of clothes in his wake in the bedroom. Does that mean he won't be coming back? Do I even care?

I check my phone but he's not sent any messages or tried to call. I can't believe he can't even be bothered to check if his pregnant wife is okay.

I change into my pyjamas and climb into bed, hoping that sleep will come but my mind is filled with images of Fran and Dom together, the baby and finally Jake.

Jake, what have I done?

∞ ∞ ∞

I wake up in the morning feeling groggy after hardly any sleep. I look at the clock. It's 10am. The events of last night have been on replay in my mind – all night.

I could just hide in bed all day, surely that would be okay but it's Christmas Day and Mum is expecting me. She'll only show up here if I don't go. I might as well get ready and I'll have to tell her what's happened. I wonder who will be more devastated, she loves Dom. I toy with the idea about telling her that I don't know who the father is. Dom seems so adamant it's not him but I feel that I really need to talk to him. Perhaps we haven't done it over the last month, he could be thinking I'm earlier than I am. I need to know. Even if he is a massive arsehole.

I get ready in my best Christmas outfit, taking care over my hair and make-up. I don't have to look like shit, even if I feel like it. I head over to Mum's ready for the onslaught, I wish I could have a drink for this. Her intentions will be good but I know it'll be exhausting having to comfort her whilst trying to deal with my own feelings.

As I tap on the door of our family home, I can't help but look over to Dom's parents' home. They won't have come over to Mum's yet. I wonder if Dom is at their house now, telling them? Maybe none of them will come over. I wish Dad was still here, his soft presence would be so nice right now, he'd know what to do. One of his hugs could make me feel so much better.

Mum pulls the door open, a glass in her hand, and wearing her gaudiest Christmas outfit yet, a red and green dress which could easily make you mistake her for Mrs Santa Claus. Mum loves Christmas and any holiday really is the perfect excuse for dressing up, eating lots and family time.

'Merry Christmas, darling!' She smiles. 'I was going to pour you one and then I remembered.' She winks. 'Come in, come in.'

'Merry Christmas, Mum.' I follow her into the hallway ready to tell all and half wishing I could have that drink to help the story out. I wonder how many Mum has had this morning, let's hope not too many as it'll make her even more emotional.

'Mu..' I begin, but before I get a chance to say anything else, I'm interrupted.

'There you are darling.' Dom's eyes flash at me, trying to give me some kind of message. What the hell is he doing here? A wave of anger hits me. The arsehole cheats on me and now he wants to play happy families.

'What the...'

Dom cuts me off, looking between Mum and me. 'We had a little tiff last night, didn't we? Let's try and forget about it today and just enjoy Christmas, shall we. We can deal with everything else *later*. Mum and Dad are through here,' he says leading me through to the living room. That's me told.

Does he expect me to pretend we're okay? After denying our baby. Although, I don't fancy making a scene in front of everyone and perhaps it would be nice just to enjoy the day and then we can talk about it all properly later this evening. I don't really want to have this fight in front of Mum, she has good intentions but she'll somehow make it all about her and I just can't cope with that, especially after last night. It would be nice not to ruin everyone's Christmas, I think back to how I ruined it last Christmas, so much pain and disappointment.

I let Dom take the lead and I can't help but marvel at it all. The lies, the charm. I'm almost sucked back in myself but one thing I cannot forget. Him lying his arse off to Fran saying the baby isn't his, is that so he can carry on his affair with her?

'How's everything in the office?' Dom's Dad, Clive asks.

I swallow down the bile that's beginning to rise at the thought of the office and Fran. 'Oh, same as usual, you know.' I smile noncommittally.

Mum starts to walk around us offering nibbles, I know lunch won't be far behind so I refuse them.

'Shall we do gifts now?' Mum asks, a look of glee on her face.

Mum clearly hasn't said anything to anyone about the baby because they'd be talking about it now. I did say to her not to tell his parents so it seems she's listened, which I'm thrilled about. There's a first time for everything.

'Perhaps we should do gifts after dinner,' I suggest, smiling sweetly. I could cry off home after lunch, feigning illness. Mum would know why but the others don't have to. This pretence is a lot to cope with.

Dom's dad tells me the ins and outs of what he's been up to now he's retired and I try to nod along kindly but I find it hard to focus on the conversation. My mind keeps returning to Dom and Fran and even though I've only been in this alternate life a week I can't help but feel devastated. It seems the grass isn't greener on the other side.

'Can everyone gather around the table please,' Mum breaks the chitchat. 'I've got crackers and a little surprise too.' She smiles, turning to me. 'I know we said we'd do presents after dinner but this one is *really* special.'

Mum fusses around everyone making sure they sit in their assigned seats, nameplates and everything. There are only five of us so really just pointing would do, but she loves to make the Christmas table special, a huge Christmas centrepiece, complete with candles, sits in the middle. I'm sat next to Dom, much to my distain.

'Does anyone need a top up of drink? Clive, Stella? Everyone needs their wine glasses filled.' She goes around taking glasses and everyone resumes chatting. Mum disappears to the kitchen and comes back in with champagne for everyone, including me. As she puts it down, she gives me a wink and I hold it up to my face smelling apple juice. She's brilliant. She thinks of everything.

'Anything planned for the new year?' Stella asks me. I think over what the next year will bring. Will I be here or will I be back with Jake? Back in my real life? My whole Dom bubble has been completely burst but we're having a baby together so perhaps we should try to make it work. That's what people do, isn't it?

'Not really. What about you?' I ask, trying to divert the attention from me.

'Well, we have the cruise at the end of January, you know that, we're just finishing preparing for it.'

'Of course.' I smile tightly. 'Remind me where you're going again?'

'It's a world cruise so all over, we're going to South America, the Caribbean and even over to Australia.' Her eyes twinkle with the excitement of it all.

'Oh yes, it sounds lovely,' I say but I'm finding it hard to inject any enthusiasm into my voice.

'I think you have a pretty exciting year ahead too though, right sweetie?' Mum smiles, she's loving knowing more than Dom's parents.

Stella looks to me for confirmation.

'Hmmm.' I nod hoping that will be the end of it. 'She means with work and everything.' I eye Mum, trying to get her to stop.

Mum taps her glass, Dom and Clive stop talking about the football and all look to Mum for the toast.

'Before I start on the toast, I have something very special I'd like to present.' She pulls out a wrapped gift. 'Stella, why don't you do the honours?' She smiles over at me.

'Oh lovely, thank you.'

As she unwraps it, I see her pull out a frame. She turns it around scrutinising the image held within. I lean over wondering what it could possibly be to see my baby scan photograph blown up to ten by eight. I look over at Mum, who's grinning ear to ear. Oh no. Dom who having registered what it is, is absolutely fuming. He looks between my mum and me.

'Is this some kind of sick joke?' he asks, standing up from the table.

Mum looks embarrassed. 'Oh, I'm so sorry dear, I thought you'd have told them by now.'

'Your mum knows?' He looks accusingly at me.

'Yes, she knows. She was with me when I found out,' I spit, matter of a fact.

'What's the matter, dear?' Stella asks. 'This is lovely news. Congratulations to you both. We were beginning to wonder if you were ever going to make us grandparents.' She gives Clive a knowing smile. 'This is a lovely way to be told,' Stella says trying to smooth the situation but I can see Dom is not having any of it.

'No, it's not Mum. It's not a nice way to be told anything. That,' he says pointing at the picture in Stella's hands, 'Is *not* my baby.'

Mum covers her mouth; she looks ready to burst into tears. Her lovely moment ruined; I almost feel sorry for her.

'Why do you keep saying that? Of course, it's your baby.' I stand up too, not wanting him to loom over me, I look him in the eye ready for a fight.

'No, it's not. I know that for a fact.'

'Why are you so sure?' I shout. 'I'm thirteen weeks along, you see it is yours.'

'No, it's not because I had a vasectomy five years ago.'

The whole table gasps.

Chapter 21

'A vasectomy?' I ask, feeling my throat tighten. 'Did I know about this?' I can't imagine not wanting children but in this strange dream perhaps I've coveted our lifestyle over a family. I involuntarily put my hand over my bump.

'Well...' Dom at least has the decency to look self-conscious.

'Did you have a secret vasectomy five years ago?' I can hardly believe the words coming out of my mouth.

'I've always been up front about not wanting kids,' Dom says, as if that makes his actions acceptable.

'But I want kids,' I yell. 'I want this kid.' My mind starts to race because if it's not Dom's, whose baby is it?

Mum starts to wail in the corner of the room, her great reveal has really not gone to plan.

Stella and Clive get up, Stella carefully places the frame back on the table.

'Thank you for your hospitality, Anna, but I think we'd better leave,' she says, looking between Dom and me. She looks utterly devastated.

Dom turns to his parents. 'I'm awfully sorry about all this. I didn't know she knew,' he explains, thrusting his finger towards Mum like it's all her fault.

His wronged man act to his parents pisses me off. I'm so sick of him pretending to be so perfect, the words slip out of my mouth before I can help it.

'Don't act all pious and blame Mum as though this mess is all her fault. You're far from perfect, you've been having an affair with Fran,' I say, looking pointedly at Clive and Stella.

Another collective gasp around the table, it's turning into a real soap opera now. Stella's face has turned puce with the embarrassment of it all. She's such a reserved person that sometimes it's hard to imagine Mum and Stella being such great friends but really, they're kindred spirits. Stella is the calm to Mum's storm. I hope this won't ruin their friendship, but I fear it will.

Dom's expression changes, his secret out he clearly no longer cares what people think of him. 'Oh, she's just the icing on the cake,' he sneers, an ugly grimace on his lips. He's always been a handsome man but I've never seen him looking so ugly. 'Why do you think I'm up in London so much?'

'But why?' I ask. 'I thought we were happy?'

'You've always continued to pine about Jake, don't think I don't know that. Regret marrying me? Well, you don't need to now. You can go and have whoever's baby that is, probably your bloody trainer's, he's always sniffing around like a huge, dumb dog.' Having had the last word, he turns and marches out of the room; it seems to be his party trick. As he reaches the door he turns.

'You'll be hearing from my solicitor and don't expect much in the settlement. I'd start job hunting too, if I were you.'

He hurries about fetching their coats whilst I try to

comfort Mum but I'm acutely aware it should be me who's being comforted. It's my husband who was having an affair and is now leaving me.

'I'm sorry, Mum, I know how much you love Dom,' I say in a small voice, suddenly ashamed of the way I behaved. I wish that Dad was here, he'd know how to deal with everything, Mum included.

'What are you talking about? I love you. Dom's okay, but if he's not making you happy and clearly having a vasectomy behind your back is wrong, very wrong, I don't want to see him ever again.' She shakes her head and I can't hide my shock. Dom's very charming and they'd always be off giggling about something or other, sometimes when we came for tea I'd feel like I was intruding into their special team of two.

'But I always kind of felt like you preferred him to me. Like the son you never had?' I admit, a bitter taste in my mouth.

'No, I liked him because he made *you* happy but I can see I've had my head in the sand and ignored things because everything was good. Truth be told I always thought he was a bit pompous and bossy but if you were happy with that, I was happy.' She offers me a small smile. 'Looks like Dad was right.'

'Dad?' I ask.

'He always thought he wasn't good enough for you. To be honest, he thought you should have married Jake.'

Tears spring to my eyes at the thought of my sweet Dad. Did he see through Dom all along?

I'm shocked to hear my mum speak like this about Dom. She's always gone on like he's so wonderful, handsome, charming and clever.

'I'm sorry about the announcement though.' She looks down, knowing her dramatics often get her into trouble. I can't blame her she is who she is and I wouldn't expect anything else.

'It's okay, you were excited.' I smile warmly at her; we might not always see eye to eye but I know she's on my side no matter what. 'If it had been Dom's baby it would probably have gone down very well.' I smile and I can't stop myself from beginning to laugh at the ridiculousness of it all. I lock eyes with Mum and she starts on the hysterics too, her belly raising up and down as she gasps for air with a silent laugh. It feels good to laugh, like a release from everything, from Dom, from Fran and finally from Jake. Jake. The image of his face pops back into my mind and he's with Jeanie and their children.

'Who's the father?' Mum looks to me, bringing me back from my thoughts. I begin to rack my brain, who is the father? Could it really be Brad? But there's no chemistry there. No attraction, not on my side anyway, though he certainly is a good-looking man. If I hadn't been so focused on Dom would I have considered him? Maybe. I've hardly been in touch with anyone else since I've been here, is there someone else out there? A one-night stand. My head feels wobbly and I can feel my breathing start to quicken.

'I'm not really sure,' I admit, looking down as I think over the last week. I can feel my breath start to quicken and I have a sudden urge to run but instead I start to cry, the hysterics of laughter have long gone and here I am sobbing uncontrollably. Now my mum holds me, just like when I was a child and I lean in because I don't have the energy to be strong for her anymore. Not for her or anyone else. It's time to put myself and this baby first, I realise. I just need to figure out who the father is.

'Just calm down love, we can figure this out. We don't need to do everything right away.'

'Okay.' I shrug trying desperately to get my breathing even. I just need to know. I need to see Brad so I can find out. I walk over to the back door and look out into the garden. What was once my happy place is so different now. Mum and Dad had the garden paved shortly after the wedding. With Dad's fading health it was just too much for him.

I try to call Brad but there's no response. Of course not, it's Christmas Day.

'Why don't you have a lie down upstairs?' Mum asks. 'Your room's made up.'

'I'd rather go home,' I say but I'm acutely aware of which home I mean and it isn't the glossy, stark one. If only I could click my red shoes together.

'Do you think Dom will be there?' Mum asks. 'Stay here, you don't need to speak to him right now. I could go and get some things for you.'

I mull over the words coming from Mum's mouth. She's right I don't want to go there now, but I can see that Dom's car is still on his parents drive, this is the only opportunity I might get without having to speak to Dom again. I don't much fancy rehashing everything with him or facing his hostility. Anyway, if I don't go now, he might lock me out.

'I'll go back and get some clothes,' I say and while I'm there I'll look for clues about anyone else I'm seeing or other contact details for Brad. Could there be a whole host of men out there for me, like Dom has a whole host of women?

Who am I here?

I'm not sure I like me.

The weather has turned, with strong winds and rain, and it takes some effort to fight my car door open. I drive slowly, my windscreen wipers are on full, thrashing wildly to keep the water off and my view clear but it's hard going. My phone beeps and I grab it, but who could it be? Jeanie and Marnie aren't my friends here, Fran isn't my friend here or anywhere for that matter. As I glance down again, I see that it's Brad. I stab at the phone whilst I'm driving, desperate to find out if the baby is his. I'm on the motorway and there's nowhere to pull over but if I just hold straight it will be okay.

'Brad?' I say, breathlessly. Is it you? Are you the Dad?

'You called?' he says monotone, I almost forgot about our terrible non-session. I wince at the thought of his sick-soaked trainers. Surely, he can't stay mad at me once he knows why? He rang me back, that's a good sign. If only I'd told him earlier, he could have told me whether it's his or asked and then I would know.

'Yes, sorry about the sick and everything,' I say, holding the steering wheel tight against the strong winds. It feels as though it could blow the car over.

'It's fine but I don't think we can continue really, you're just not into it anymore, are you?' he says in a kinder tone and I feel myself warm to him. No wonder he acted so upset if we'd be carrying on and I've cancelled or forgotten sessions and generally been crap to him. Perhaps it won't be so bad, he seems like a caring kind of guy, even if he isn't the person I envisioned myself with.

'I'm pregnant,' I say, not wanting to prolong the agony any longer, waiting for the pin to drop and for him to know that it's his or *possibly* his. Will he be happy? Sad? Angry?

'Congratulations! I must say it explains a lot about the sick on my shoe,' he says. 'I thought you'd been drinking, but I'm pleased to hear that, send my congratulations to Dom as well. You know we could do pregnancy appropriate lessons.' He begins to ramble on whilst I furiously try to control the car. I slow right down because trying to concentrate on everything is making my head hurt.

'No, Brad. I'm telling you because I think it might be your baby.' I'm surprised it's not the first thought that occurred to him, he's not even asked.

Brad begins to laugh. 'You're hilarious,' he says. 'Is pregnancy making you loopy? You're definitely not drinking, are you?' Concern comes into his voice.

'No, look Brad I know it's not Dom's because he's had a vasectomy, so it might be yours,' I explain desperately. Why isn't he getting it? A huge curve in the road is coming up and my windscreen wipers are still thrashing wildly against the rain pelting down.

'Have you been talking to Tom? You two think you're so funny.'

'Who's Tom? No Brad, I really think it might be yours.'

'I can tell you it's not, darling, for a fact,' he says bluntly. There's still a hint of humour in his voice and I can't work out what's so funny.

Why does no one seem to want to take responsibility for this baby. All I know is that it wasn't an immaculate conception, whoever's it is. 'I don't understand, Brad, it really could be yours.'

'I always assumed you knew; Tom isn't just a man I live with he's my boyfriend. I'm gay Lena. We've never had sex. You sound so weird; do you need some help?'

'No. Bye.' I drop the phone and begin to accelerate again, desperate to get back to the house for clues.

I'm stunned, so it really isn't Brad's or Dom's. I can hear Eli's voice in my head and his assumptions nearly every man is gay. One thing's for sure, I need to improve my gaydar.

I try to control the car around the bend but I've accelerated too much whilst talking to Brad and the car is shaking. The phone falls down under the passenger seat and, stupidly, I go to grab it. As I sit back up I realise I've made a grave mistake, I'm heading for a tree. I try to turn the wheel, try to steer away from it, try my best. What's a tree doing so close to the motorway anyway?

I can't avoid it. It's too late. Then everything goes black.

Chapter 22

I awake to the familiar sound of a chainsaw. I've heard it so many times before whilst Jake cuts up wood in the garden. I shake my head and I can feel an acute pain in my neck. I open my eyes and I'm sitting in my car; the rain has eased but I can see the winds are still here. I go to move again but I'm stuck, the airbag is in my face. I hear a screaming sound over and over it takes a long while to realise, it's me.

'It's okay, it's okay,' says a soothing male voice, I try to turn my head but I can't locate the owner of the voice. 'You've had a little accident. Fortunately, the tree has fallen on the back of the car, we're just trying to move it so we can set you free,' he continues. Tree? My head feels groggy.

'Shouldn't be long,' he says, trying to reassure me.

Finally, after what feels like an eternity the chainsaw stops. I watch through the window; the firefighters have a discussion with the man with the chainsaw who then comes running over to the door.

'Lena?' His brown eyes bore into mine and it feels as though he sees me for the first time in a long time.

'Jake?'

'Lena, my darling. You're going to be okay. We're

just getting you out.' My darling?

The firefighters take over and they lift me from the car. I feel stiff and bruised. My hand goes to my stomach, stroking it brings me comfort but as something begins to niggle at me, I begin to hyperventilate.

'Don't worry, honey. I'm here.' Jake's back at my side, trying to hold my hand, searching my face to see I'm okay.

'My baby. My baby.' I clutch my stomach. Please let the baby be okay.

'Baby?' Jake asks reaching for my hand again.

'What are you doing,' I say, shrugging him away as they roll me into the ambulance.

'Trying to hold your hand. You've had a nasty shock. You must've been so scared,' he says, kindly. 'I'll travel with her, I'm her husband,' he says, turning his attention to the paramedic.

What? I'm back? I've woken up? What about the baby? I start to spiral, something I'd wanted for so long and it was so close and now what? I start to sob at the thought and I can feel Jake's hand on my back trying to soothe me but he doesn't understand. It's another loss but this one wasn't even real, that dream was long and so real, and an emotional rollercoaster.

I had everything I ever wanted. Almost.

I'm back in the hospital and I can't stop crying. Jake has barely been able to get a word out of me except baby. The doctor comes in.

'Well it looks like you're very lucky. The way you turned, means the tree struck the car at the back and it completely avoided you so apart from a few scratches and bruises and a bit of whiplash on your neck everything looks good. I've arranged a scan for the baby.'

Jake moves forward. 'Baby?' He grins from ear to ear.

'There's no baby. I think I was dreaming.' I shrug at Jake; a huge sad sigh escapes my lips and I cover my face with my hands so I don't have to watch the disappointment on his face. The one I've seen before, so many times.

The doctor looks between us, puzzled. 'I'm not sure about your dreams,' he says. 'But your blood test indicates you're pregnant, we'll know more once you have the scan.'

My mind is blown but I don't dare hope too hard, I've been disappointed so many times before. It feels weird having Jake so close to me again. I look at him with different eyes now and I wonder whether we even belong together. I don't feel any electricity or excitement like I did when Dom touched me, but is that normal with time? Jake starts to get excited and it's the most animated I've seen him in a long time. Will this baby fix our relationship? Then I remember Jake with Jeanie and how they seemed so happy together. Them and their little family.

∞ ∞ ∞

The nurse comes in and leads us up to the second floor for a scan.

'All being well you can be discharged after this.' She smiles and leaves us in another room with a monitor.

As the sonographer pulls up my top she laughs, I'm taken aback. What's there to laugh at? Does she already know there's no baby and she finds it funny?

'Do you have other children?' she asks, smiling.

'No,' I say, looking at Jake, puzzled by the question. Maybe it's my body, does it look like I have carried other children?

She looks between us and senses my unease.

'Sorry,' she says. 'It's just this being stuck above your bellybutton made me laugh.' As she says it, she puts her hand out and hands me a small, green Christmas tree. Penny's Christmas tree. I stare at it for perhaps longer than necessary and place it back into my pocket for Penny.

The doctor coats my stomach with the gel and I grab hold of Jake's hand. I'm home but I feel so different in myself, I look back down at the soft rolls around my tummy and I don't feel distaste any longer. I know I can look different; I know I can work hard and I hope this body will allow me to carry this baby.

The doctor quietly looks at the scan, and the silence is deafening. I hold my breath hoping for good news but almost expecting bad.

'Is this your first scan?' she asks, sensing my nerves.

I go to say 'no' but Jake answers 'No,' over me. We lock eyes, our shared sadness over our lost babies will always link us. The doctor is quiet, concentrating on our scan.

'Looks like you're around thirteen weeks, did you not know?' she finally asks, puzzled by my odd behaviour.

'My periods have been all over the place for a while so I guess I didn't notice. Is the baby okay?' I ask tentatively.

'They look fine to me; do you want to listen to the heartbeats?'

'They?' I ask.

'Yes, there are two in there.' She smiles.

I cover my mouth with my hand, I'm shocked. I can feel Jake hold his breath; this was the point last time where we knew. No heartbeat. Suddenly we can hear a rapid little beat, then another, there they are and they're perfect. I smile and look up at Jake, he's beaming from ear to ear and I allow myself to imagine it will be okay, we can be happy together. I still can't help but think of Jake with Jeanie, I'd never considered them a match but even I can't deny they had chemistry and they seemed happy together. Was he happier with her than with me? I'm almost pissed off with Jake and I have to remind myself that it's not his fault, it was a silly dream. If I told Jeanie she would laugh, but I won't tell her.

∞ ∞ ∞

'I'm so thrilled about the babies,' Jake says, putting his hand over mine as we start to drive home. 'That's the best Christmas present a guy could wish for. Shall we tell our parents on Christmas day?'

I blink, Christmas day?

'What day is it?' I ask, I feel like the world has been turned upside down again.

'It's Christmas Eve silly, but as the baby's over the twelve-week part we could tell them?'

I imagine telling Mum again, this time it could be so different. No big show, it could be really lovely. And twins. How did another baby get in there? Then I think of telling Jake's mum, will she finally accept me, will I finally be good enough now I'm carrying not one but two of her son's babies.

'Sounds like a good idea,' I say quietly. Not wanting to cause a fight, it's nice to be back on good terms. I'm thrilled that the babies are his, he's a good man but I can't help feeling differently about him. We've been coasting for a long time and I'm not happy in this relationship. It's crystal clear to me now. I think back to all the bickering and sniping, how tiring it was and how that's not what I want our babies to see. I may not have been entirely myself in the Dom world but there were things about me that I did like, I had goals and I wasn't just coasting along in a dead-end job, I put myself first, perhaps a little too much but here it hasn't felt like that in a long time.

∞ ∞ ∞

'You've been very quiet,' Jake notes as we slump on the sofa. Spence has jumped up to be with us and his head is on my lap, protectively. When I came into the house, he was so excited it was as though he hadn't seen me for weeks. I felt exactly the same way.

I stroke his soft fur, I'm so happy to be back in his soothing company and push thoughts of horrible Ginger out of my mind, that cat really hated me.

'I know,' I say and look into Jake's eyes. So kind and lovely but I have no doubts about the future. The future I want. 'I'm looking forward to telling everyone about the babies tomorrow,' I say.

'Me too. They'll be so excited for us.'

'They will. They will.'

Would it be kinder to tell him now, or wait until after Christmas? I'm torn. I don't want to hurt him but it's almost unavoidable.

Chapter 23

One year later

'Merry Christmas my little angels.' Mum puts her arms out to take Noah from me. Nicholas is sat on my other hip, such a mummy's boy, Mum knows there's no chance he'll go to her straight away. He has to warm up, unlike his brother.

Noah's grinning from ear to ear, the happiest baby I've ever seen, his golden ringlets bouncing around as he jiggles excitedly. I hand him over and he immediately grabs hold of Mum's hair in a vicelike grip, I laugh knowing that he'll be pulling a handful of that out any minute.

'Ouch. Those little mitts are nasty,' Mum says, laughing as she unfurls his little hands. Mum looks behind me to Nicholas hiding his face in my shoulder.

'I know,' I say, laughing along with her. I'm surprised I have any hair left.

'Hello, young Nicholas,' she says, giving him a big grin. It only makes him hide further. 'Wow, his hair's really growing in now, look how dark it is.' She marvels at it while stroking his head.

I often get comments about the twins, because they

look so different. Noah is blonde hair and blue eyed, he had a mass of hair straight away which has grown into the most beautiful, blonde curls. Whereas Nicholas was born bald with dark, almost black eyes, I always thought babies were born with blue eyes but not in this case. Now his hair is finally growing in I can already feel it's a coarser texture than Noah's, and it's so dark it makes them look worlds apart. He looks a lot like Jake, they even have a matching dimple.

Mum pops Noah down onto the floor and he immediately starts shuffling around, he's not crawling yet but he's close and gets so frustrated when he can't get over to something he wants. I place Nicholas down by his side and he reaches his podgy arms back up to me, not ready to go down on the floor yet. I pick him up and place him on my knee. I pop some toys down in front of Noah and he immediately starts to throw everything around.

Mum smiles as she watches the boys then turns her attention to me. 'Is everything settled with the office now?'

'Yes, I think so. I should get my pay out soon, I need to wait a few more months.' I smile, finding myself looking towards his parents' house. I wonder if he's over there now for Christmas lunch? Dom.

I haven't seen him since my last day in the office and we never mentioned the kiss. We both knew it was inappropriate. I'm sure I wasn't the only one he tried it on with, there were plenty of rumours. Looks as though Eli was right about Dom being an international playboy.

It turned out that there were a number of complaints against Dom, including one surrounding my interview for the management position that was being investigated. Apparently, a few of the other interviewers' thought Dom had purposefully given me very low scores and even though they were happy with Kian and it would have been close, the others on the panel felt that I hadn't been fairly interviewed.

Dom's still working there, I don't know what he said or who he slept with to keep his job but it didn't surprise me. It didn't really bother me either. He's so high up in the company that he's probably integral to its success, though Mum's convinced he'll be quietly got rid of eventually. I don't know, and I don't think I care either.

'You should probably start looking for something soon, your maternity pay must be coming to an end? Even with the extra bit of money from your redundancy you'll need something.' Mum smiles, I know she's been worrying about me and what I'm going to do next but she doesn't know how well work paid me off, I'll be alright for a bit longer.

An alarm goes off and Mum excuses herself to go to the kitchen to check on the roast. Nicholas is finally warmed up enough to go down on the floor and I place him next to his brother.

Mum flounces back into the living room. 'Wine?' she asks, glass in hand, decision already made. 'And I hope you've brought your appetite? I've done way too much for the five of us. They'll eat some of it, right?'

'Oh yes, especially Noah, he loves his food. They'll just have the vegetables though.' I smile.

'And you?' she checks.

'Yes, I'll have plenty.' I roll my eyes; this isn't the first time we've had this conversation and it's wearing thin.

'You're just so tiny now.' She gestures wildly at my

figure. 'You wouldn't think you'd had two children nearly seven months ago.' She appraises me as she says it and I can see the concern in her eyes.

I shrug. 'That's because I've been looking after myself Mum and working out. I'm eating a well-balanced diet and I was breastfeeding and that helps mums lose weight. Don't worry so much.'

She gives me a curt nod. 'Are you still doing that Mum fitness class thing?'

'Yes, FitMums. It's great because I can take the boys with me and they can play with the other kids. I love it and so do they. Well Nicholas doesn't always, but he's getting better at it.' I stroke his hair as I say his name, looking at my sweet, sensitive boy. 'Although, Silvey who runs the class is pregnant and will be going on maternity leave soon.' I gear up to asking Mum. 'She's asked if I'd step in actually, she says there's some training.' I give a tight smile; I'm really excited by the idea but I don't want Mum getting carried away. 'Do you think you could look after the boys whilst I trained?' I've been working up to asking her for a few weeks, I don't know why I've been putting it off, not wanting her theatrics.

'Sure, I can.' Mum smiles.

A gawdy Christmas tune interrupts us, it's Mum's doorbell, she switches to that tune every Christmas. We both know who it is.

'Merry Christmas, Anna. Where are they?' Jake singsongs.

'Through here.' Mum leads Jake through to the living room, Spence bouncing around in his wake. In the living room he scoups both boys into his arms, covering them in kisses while Spence yaps at his heels. His hair looks longer than the last time I saw him. He has a new kind of ease about him and I've noticed he smiles more often or maybe that's just when I see him with the boys. There's been a particular spring in his step recently.

'Lena.' He nods and smiles in my direction but doesn't make an attempt to kiss me. 'How have my boys been?' he asks, bringing his attention back to them. 'Have you been good for your mama?'

He's a great father, I knew he would be and I think it's better this way, tougher at times, maybe, especially for me, but better. When I think back to this time last year, it seems like another life, though not the strange one with Dom.

I waited until Boxing Day to bring it up. It had been hard not to say anything on Christmas Day but we wanted to tell our parents so I bit my tongue, but I couldn't let it continue past that.

'I think we should take a break,' I said when we were alone in our own home.

He looked at me bemused. 'What? We're about to have twins.'

'Yes, and that won't change, you'll be as involved as ever but I'm not happy. I haven't been for a long time and neither have you. I choose me and I choose these babies but I don't know if I choose our relationship and I feel like I need time to think about it all and you deserve that too. I've lost so much of myself over the last few years.'

'I never asked you to change anything about yourself,' Jake started, defensively, his neck muscles clenching with tension.

I felt relief; this conversation had been a long time coming and I don't know why I left it so long. Perhaps we could have worked it out sooner, or perhaps we could have moved on from each other sooner, but it doesn't matter because we have a bond for life now, in the form of the little babies that were growing in my stomach.

'I know you never asked, but I did it anyway. I used to love to keep fit and now I never do anything, I never have the drive and I have spent so much of my energy feeling irritated with you, bickering with you and now I want to concentrate on me. I want us to be the best parents ever but it doesn't have to be together. It might be, but I think it might not be. I'm sorry.'

He started to nod and tears filled his eyes, but *I* didn't cry. I sat and held him, let him shed his silent tears. This had been a long time coming for me and I felt confident in my decision. It was time to work on ourselves, so we could be amazing co-parents to our miracle babies.

We agreed as this is their first Christmas, we wanted to spend it together. After the initial untangling of our lives a new calm ensued in which not only I but Jake realised we were better apart. The boys are happy living between us and we're bossing this co-parenting business, even if I do say so myself.

'They're good, Nicholas isn't sleeping well though. I think I may need to take him for a walk after lunch so he'll go down,' I say, smiling at my little boy.

∞ ∞ ∞

A few hours later and following a severe overindulge during lunch, I wrap myself and Nicholas up, fighting him into his snowsuit. I stuff my bag in the other side of the double buggy. Noah will sleep better in the cot so I'm not going to take him too, Jake will put him down before he heads to his parents for the rest of Christmas day. Mum can pop her feet up for a little bit. I plan my route in my head, straight down the path and around the park four or five times should do it. It's cold, crisp and bright so I make sure I pop hats on both of us. I can see Nicholas' eyes already starting to flutter, I just need to walk and he'll be out for an hour or two and hopefully sleep through the night.

As I walk along the path, I enjoy the fresh air. It'll be nice to have a bit of a walk and let my huge Christmas dinner go down. As I round the park, I enjoy its beauty. There's a sprinkling of snow which makes it feel so Christmassy. I could almost break into a run but I don't. I breath the cool air in and let it fill my lungs. I'm so much calmer now I don't work at Morgans. I go to the FitMums classes three times a week and I love it, especially as there's a free creche. FitMums helps quiet my busy mind but also has helped me get back into shape and do something for myself. For that short time, I'm not just a Mum. I'm excited at the prospect of taking over the classes from Silvey but I'm nervous. Some of the other mums have been going longer than me but I'm the only one who goes regularly, I never miss a session. Silvey said my enthusiasm and dedication made me the perfect candidate. She hadn't even asked anyone else. I'm secretly hoping I can make a career out of it. I don't want to tell Mum yet because she'll get all carried away and before I know it I'll come home to banners congratulating me on my new job when it's just a bit of maternity cover really. For now.

As I round the corner of the park for the third time, I see him. He wasn't there the last time I went round and I think about turning back. It's not that I don't want to talk to him, but it could be a bit awkward. As I hesitate in the path, looking down at Nicholas' sleeping face, he spots me.

'Lena, Lena?' he calls, getting up off the bench and heading over to me.

'I thought it was you.' He smiles and readjusts his new glasses, they're a lot nicer and frame his face really well. It's been a while since we've seen each other. Eight months to be exact, when I last worked at Morgans.

'Hey, Kian.' I smile back awkwardly. I don't know what he knows about the reasons around me leaving.

'How have you been? Look at him, he's so cute.' Kian lowers his voice as he notices Nicholas sleeping.

'Yes, good. And you? How's work? Do you live around here?'

Kian nods. 'Just moved, I live a few streets over that way.' He points, indicating the opposite direction to Mum's.

'Wow, it doesn't seem long ago you moved here for your girlfriend and you're moving again? Something bigger?' I'm wondering if they've got some of their own news.

Kian looks somewhat embarrassed. 'Smaller actually.' He looks down. 'We broke up, it wasn't working out. I'm just renting a flat for now, whilst I decide what I want to do.'

'Oh right, sorry.' How awful to move country for someone and for it not to work out. 'Are some of your family over for Christmas?' I change tack, feeling bad for making him feel worse and on Christmas Day too, the poor guy.

He shakes his head and looks down.

'Are you all alone?' I've made it worse.

He nods and I feel incredibly sad for him. 'I was

supposed to spend it with Steph but obviously we broke up and I just didn't fancy going home and talking about it all over Christmas. I thought it wouldn't be so bad…' he trails off. Poor guy.

'How's work?' I ask the inevitable question.

'Well there's been a lot of change but you probably know all about that?' A small smile plays on his lips.

'A lot of change?' I take the bait and can't help wondering what could have changed. Perhaps they've replaced me. I'm surprised Eli hasn't filled me in on all the gossip, he'd normally love that. Come to think of it, I did have a few missed calls from him. I resolve to call him back soon.

'Dom's gone.' Kian announces and I gasp, I watch my breath rise up in the cool air.

'Really?' I squeak. Do I have anything to do with this?

'Yes, well it all went off, he had been sleeping with one of the new clients and she caught him in bed with Fran. Everyone was shocked. They're still deciding what to do about Fran because she wasn't sleeping with a client, I think it's a bit more unclear but the client is fuming. She's dropped us.'

I put my hand over my mouth and muffle my laughter, the idea of Dom being caught with his pants down is so funny, he just can't help himself.

'Yes, it was quite the scandal at work, Fran's not been in the office since just been sending emails to direct everyone. Oh, I didn't tell you the best bit. She was dressed head to toe in some kind of tight PVC bondage gear, it was quite distressing for the client apparently.'

I let out a loud cackle, I can't hold it in. Kian's smiling now from ear to ear, it's good to see him cheer up.

My cackle was a bit too loud and wakes up Nicholas and he begins to wail.

'I better go,' I say. Desperate to get back to the house before he gets too loud. I look up at Kian, his face has fallen and I see how sad his eyes are. Before I know it, I find myself saying. 'I'm going to my friend's house for Boxing Day drinks tomorrow, why don't you join us?'

'Really? That would be great.' He pulls out a card with the Morgans' logo on it and hands it to me. 'It has my mobile number on it,' he says in answer to my frown.

'I'll message you the address.' I head off with Nicholas, crying all the way home.

Chapter 24

'So, when does Lena's BOYFRIEND arrive?' Marnie teases. We're all gathered at Marnie's in true Boxing Day tradition and I reflect on how different my life is now. The boys are at Jake's for the night so it's just me, Marnie, Mitch and Jeanie. Dana's fast asleep in bed but Penny is skipping around skirting bedtime and insisting on greeting all the guests before she goes up. I think she's secretly hoping Kian will bring her a gift, she's going to be sorely disappointed.

'He's not my boyfriend.' I'm beginning to wish I hadn't invited Kian now. 'I just felt for him, I think he's spent Christmas all alone. What was I supposed to do?'

Jeanie nods. 'I know I'm always inviting random men to this too, they just never come.' She laughs at her own joke, shaking her boho hair and readjusting her dress.

∞ ∞ ∞

There's a sharp rap on the door and Penny bounces into action, running at full speed to it.

'Wait for me, I'll open the door,' shouts Marnie. I follow them through and hover behind Marnie and

Penny suddenly feeling nervous. Perhaps this wasn't such a good idea.

'Thank you for having me,' Kian says to Marnie in his lovely Irish accent.

'Auntie Lena has a boyfriend,' Penny starts to chant happily, having obviously listened to our conversation.

'Don't worry about that little monkey,' I say giving her the eye to stop singing.

'Did you really spend Christmas alone? Were you naughty or something?' Penny asks, clearly, she took in a lot more of that conversation than any of us realised, I must remember to watch what I say around her *and* the boys.

Kian looks at me, I suddenly feel awful for talking about him but I can see there's amusement in his eyes. 'I was very naughty last year. I didn't get a single present from Santa. That's why it's so important to remember to be a good girl. Have you been a good girl?'

Penny nods fiercely. He looks towards Marnie for confirmation.

'Well she was but she's not going to bed right now.' Marnie smiles, taking the bait.

'Oh dear, well you know I heard Santa took someone's presents away for that. I bet you have some lovely presents.'

Another big nod from Penny and she turns to Marnie. 'I want to go to bed now. I'm tired and I don't want Santa to take my presents back.'

'Can you come every bedtime?' Marnie laughs at Penny's change of heart.

Kian laughs. 'I'm going to be a really good boy now so I can have presents next year.' He grins at Penny.

Marnie is beaming. The idea of Penny going to bed

before eight on Boxing Day has filled her with joy and I can tell that she already likes Kian, maybe it won't be so bad having him here.

'Can Auntie Lena put me to bed please, Mummy?' she asks in her sweetest voice. How can I say no?

'Better ask Auntie Lena,' Marnie gestures to me.

'Please, Auntie Lena,' Penny whines, tugging on my arms.

'Okay, okay. You don't mind do you Kian?' I feel bad leaving him as soon as he arrives.

'He's fine,' Penny dismisses him before he has a chance to answer and Kian nods along following Marnie through to the living room. He's just a friend but I feel nervous for him having to mix with my friends without me. What will they be saying to him?

I take Penny's little hand and we go up into her room.

'You can read me two stories and then sing my songs,' Penny informs me. 'I know which stories I want.' She runs over to her bookcase and starts to ruffle through them.

'Okay, they can't be too long though. I need to check on Kian.'

'Why?' Penny asks and I can already feel this is going to take a while.

'Well, I invited him, so it's polite,' I try to explain.

'Why?' she asks again, her little face trying to work out what I'm going on about.

'Never mind, where are these stories?' I change the subject.

'I have something for you first.' She runs off and starts to rummage in her ottoman. I think back to a year ago when she came to me with the little cracker that changed my whole world. Finally, she pulls out a piece of paper and runs back over to me.

'Here.' She thrusts it at me and turns her attention to her books.

I gaze at the picture. She's drawn a large green Christmas tree and stuck lots of sequins onto it. As I go to open it something falls out from the open card and I bend down to collect it. As I grab at it Penny jumps in. 'That's not for you, you've had your turn.'

'Okay.' I shrug puzzled by what it is. She opens her hand and there is the little green Christmas tree sequin. 'Oh, yes. You better put that somewhere safe,' I say wondering what she meant by that. Could she know, surely not?

∞ ∞ ∞

Half an hour later and Penny's in bed. I head downstairs and I can hear Kian's soft Irish accent and Marnie and Jeanie laughing. Our guest is obviously a hit.

'What're you all laughing about?' I ask, heading over and sitting myself beside Kian.

'I was just telling them about mine and Steph's sad end.' He hangs his head down when he says it but I can see there's a smile in his eyes.

'Oh yeah?' I can feel myself sitting on the edge of my seat, I wanted to ask but thought it would be a bit intrusive. I bet the girls asked and didn't worry about such an intrusion.

'Steph's a teacher, I came home early from work one lunchtime and found her in bed with her trainee teaching assistant. He was only nineteen. It was a bit of work experience for him to really see if that's what he wants to do.'

175

Marnie and Jeanie start to laugh again and I look at my friends, embarrassed.

'I don't think it's a laughing matter,' I admonish them.

'It's fine.' Kian smiles at me.

'You haven't told her the best bit.'

'Oh yeah, when I found them in bed, the little shit, I say little, but he's taller than me with a full facial beard. He jumps out of bed and then tries to climb out of the window likes he's in some kind of ridiculous teen movie. Halfway through the bloody giant gets stuck and then bursts into tears. I kind of felt sorry for the guy, he was only a kid really. I had to help the kid out while he cried and apologised to me. I ended up feeling worse for him than me.'

I start to laugh, the thought of this nineteen-year-old giant stuck in the window is hilarious. 'What did Steph do?' I ask.

'Oh, it gets better, she left. I don't even know when because I was so distracted by him. The poor guy. Anyway, he apologised to me when I finally got him free, I think he might even lodge a complaint but I said that was up to him.'

'Wow, you're a better man than me.' Mitch laughs. 'I'd *want* him to lodge a complaint, she shouldn't get away with that.'

Kian shrugs. 'I don't think things were really right between us since I moved here, it was going to happen eventually although I don't agree with how she did it.' He's very matter of a fact about it and it's clear he has processed everything and dealt with it.

'So why did you spend Christmas alone?' Jeanie asks and I shoot her a look. Since when did everyone think it was okay to be so brazen?

'My mum was really expecting a proposal around now.' He holds his hands up. 'Not that I have indicated that at all. I didn't want to be surrounded by the questions; I wasn't going to tell them the story about what happened. I will go home in a few months; tell them we've split. I just didn't want to see all the happy couples; you know.' He shrugs.

I know exactly how he feels, when Jake and I took a break and subsequently broke up everyone was constantly asking about it. Was I sure? What about the babies? But I knew. They say when you know, you know.

The rest of the evening goes by in a blur of wine, laughter and food. It's a fun, festive evening and everyone's in good spirits. Kian is actually a real hoot; I didn't really have much time with him before I left and I'm happy to be able to spend a bit of time with him in a new way. I find myself glancing at him, he's quite good looking really and sweet. I must be getting drunk.

∞ ∞ ∞

'I'm going to head off now,' I announce to a round of boos and protests. 'I know, I know but it's late and I have the boys tomorrow and I need to get some sleep or I'll feel like crap. It's not easy to deal with two demanding babies normally, never mind hungover.'

Everyone begins to nod and we start the chorus of hugs and kisses before I leave.

Kian jumps up. 'I can give you a lift back.' He smiles.

'Thank you that would be lovely,' I agree, feeling a little hot at the thought of sitting in such close proximity to him, just the two of us. The wine must be really going to my head.

On our way back in the car Kian switches on the

radio, Mariah Carey is singing *All I Want for Christmas is You* at the top of her lungs and I sneak a sideways peak at Kian. He's really quite cute and the more he talks with that hot, Irish accent the hotter he gets.

'Stop breathing so much, you're fogging up my windscreen,' he jokes and I give him a little nudge and giggle.

As Kian pulls over, he locks eyes with me, I stare back and we don't say a word but it feels really intense, or is it just the drink? Not that Kian has been drinking.

'I don't suppose you fancy going out for dinner or drinks sometime? With me?' he asks shyly.

I smile, I feel like the cat that got the cream this Christmas.

'I'd love to.'

Life is falling into place. I might not be with Dom or Jake, but I've found me again.

And now I have a date with a hot Irish man.

The End.

Other books by Amelia Watchman

9 781913 807054